THE
HERMIT'S HORSE

DIANA PULLEIN-THOMPSON

D1324754

Armada

First published in Armada 1974 by
William Collins Sons & Co. Ltd.,
14 St. James's Place, London S.W.1.

© Diana Pullein-Thompson 1974

Printed in Great Britain by
Love & Malcomson Ltd.,
Brighton Road, Redhill, Surrey.

CHAPTER ONE

A FEW years ago we lived in a small red brick house with dormer windows, in a lane leading to hop fields, oast houses, orchards and hazel trees. In summer the high green banks were bright with violets and primroses, cow's parsley, meadowsweet and lady's slipper and countless other wildflowers whose names we did not know.

Halfway down the lane a hump-backed bridge spanned a brown stream lively with fish and, farther on, an ivy-clad house stood in a forsaken garden beside a field of rank grass, in which two dead trees, white as skeletons, looked heavenwards. It was a house everyone appeared to want, for it seemed to cry out either for restoration or demolition, to be cherished or destroyed, and in our village opinion was split on what its fate should be. Some saw a smiling old house lovingly repainted, a tidy green field, a barn converted to garage three cars; and others saw in its place neat bungalows for retired people or rows of linked houses for the newly marrieds, faced with white boards and with smooth, pocket-handkerchief gardens flanked by conifers foreign to the district.

We loved the mystery of its neglect and sometimes Sophie, my sister, and I would cycle down to the house and stand outside rudely staring in at the windows hoping to see the owner, who was known locally as the "Hermit". Once we caught sight of his thatch of thick, grey hair and his forehead pale as his barkless trees. But he never came out, not even on the warmest days, and all around the house the weeds grew thick and tall, choking the flowers which had once spread like the spillings of a paintbox across the now neglected garden.

Strange stories abound about those who take to their houses and shun the world, and our parents did not like us stopping by the house, being afraid that the Hermit was dangerously mad. But the fascination and the mystery were for us too great. Bored with home life, which seemed to revolve round our younger brother and sister, we never passed without pausing, for there was no visible danger to convince us of our parents' wisdom and our obedience in small matters was not absolute. Besides, the tangled garden where the weeds struggled for supremacy attracted all sorts of wild life. We had seen weasles with beady eyes passing softly through the grass, a goldcrest perched on a rotten gatepost, and a treecreeper hardly visible against the gnarled trunk of an ancient oak. Sometimes we heard in the dark copse behind the house the tapping of woodpeckers boring out a cavern for their nest, and one grey Sunday Sophie swore she saw a polecat crawling through the undergrowth.

It was on a Sunday in late winter that we put crisps in our cycle bags and chocolate in our pockets and set off down the lane to see our friends, the Langtons, who lived on a farm and were lucky enough to own two ponies called Mustard and Cress.

We raced over the hump-backed bridge and then slowed down as usual as we drew near the Hermit's house. We trailed our feet in the dust; our hands cold on the handle bars and a tingle in our toes. We glanced up at the dirty windows half hidden by the ivy and down at the front door, which was always shut and then, turning our heads to look across the field, silver and hard with frost, we both simultaneously cried "Wow!" and "Golly!" There, dozing by one of the skeleton trees, was a dark bay horse bright as a polished conker with large eyes and a head

6

which looked as though it had been carved from a block of wood.

"The Hermit has bought a horse!" exclaimed Sophie, who always speaks before she thinks.

"How could he?" I asked sceptically. "He never goes out; he never spends money. He's a recluse. Well, isn't he?"

"It's a stray then," said Sophie; "and needs to be rescued."

"We're dreaming," I said. "I simply don't believe it."

We threw down our cycles and pinched ourselves, but the horse was still there afterwards, and he was real. We could see his breath like steam in the fresh February air.

"Someone must feed it," said Sophie, who was eleven then with straw-coloured hair, bright wind-whipped cheeks, short straight nose and middling blue eyes. "Otherwise we must save it."

I leaned over the gate which had been mended many times with wire, and the horse stirred and swished his tail lazily; he eyed us thoughtfully raising his noble head, which would have looked well on a coin, and then tossing his mane as though saying to himself, "Children again, well who cares?"

"Do you hear, Matthew? We must save it from the Hermit's clutches."

"Oh Sophie, you nincompoop! I'm not deaf. It isn't *it*, it's *he*."

Girls, I thought, always talk too much. There are times when silence is better when decisions have to be made. I pushed my spectacles back on my nose, looked more carefully at the horse, which had now moved one cautious step in our direction.

"Must be sixteen hands or thereabouts," I added.

"Big enough for the Hermit," said Sophie.

"But we don't know his size," I objected. "We've only seen his head at a window."

For a moment I was irritated again, wanting to silence her, for she was always so sure of herself, always so quick to jump to conclusions and make decisions when I, as the eldest by two years, should have been the leader, and this caused us to quarrel.

But now this bright Sunday morning, with the last of the frost still hoary on the hedges, we were united. We climbed over the gate and patted the horse who nuzzled our hair and ran his lips over our cold faces. There was something kind about his expression, the softness in his eyes and his rather clumsy handsomeness. We didn't want to leave him; we forgot about the Langtons and their ponies, the crisps in our bags and the hands of our watches moving on and on eating up the day. We ran our hands down the horse's legs finding a bump here and a bump there.

"He's got a splint," said Sophie, "and he's had a fair number of knocks. Look at this scar."

We touched in turn a ridge of proud flesh where a deep cut had once seared the dark skin around the fetlock. We looked at his profile as he stared across the field at some animal rustling in the rank grass by the chicken house.

"His nose is Roman," I said. "See how it curves? He's a great horse."

We had ridden little but learned a great deal from the Langtons, who were pony mad, and Sophie, right in the middle of a pony book phase, spending all her packet money on paperbacks, yearned for a pony or horse to groom and care for as well as to ride.

Our thoughts were interrupted by the creaking of a window. We looked up and saw an opening in the ivy, which ran rampant over the old brick and flint house, and in the opening was the Hermit's head; his tusk-white face and his

8

eyes a cool blue like beach pebbles faded by sun. I half expected him to be wearing a nightcap, like Uncle Ebeneezer in the novel, *Kidnapped*, for he was said to be a miser. But his head was bare apart from its thick hedge of hair; his pale hands waved.

"What are you doing in my field? Out!"

His voice was hoarse, rusty for want of use, but his face was strong like the horse's face with a nose that would have looked well on a general.

"We've found a horse!" I called.

"He's fantastic," Sophie said. "I am sorry if we frightened you."

"He's great," I added, "and he seemed to want to speak to us. Is he yours?"

"Came yesterday," said the man. "Hold on a minute; I'll come down."

"Perhaps we ought to go," suggested Sophie nervously. "You know what Mum said. Supposing he's a maniac? Supposing he grabs children and hurts them, assaults them or something?"

"There's two of us against one," I reminded her, "and he's weak from lack of exercise. Didn't you notice his skin? Chalk white."

Now the man was at the door beckoning with one pale finger. He wore an old grey sweater and baggy trousers, which must have been in fashion years earlier.

We left the horse and walked within a couple of yards of the Hermit.

"As a matter of fact I could do with a little help," he said, after clearing his throat. "I could pay you a bit for it. I am not asking you a favour."

Transistor radios, a tape recorder, a book on ships, a learned zoological encyclopaedia danced for one moment before my eyes, but Sophie said:

"Oh no, we don't want money. If it's anything to do

with the horse we'll gladly work for nothing. We love horses."

The man's faded blue eyes seemed to brighten a little; his nose became almost bird-like.

"I was the same once," he said. "Used to ride in the old days before the war—different then. Not many cars. Drivers used to get down off their steamrollers to lead your pony by if it was frightened. Most people had worked with horses some time or other then. Plenty of milk floats and coal carts were still pulled by horses. That was in the thirties."

"Then we have something in common," said Sophie, with false brightness. "That's great."

"Have you hay for the horse? Where's he come from? What's his name?" It was time I thought to get down to facts.

The Hermit said: "You see I can't go out. It's my heart, dicky. I should fall down dead. I know I should," and I noticed then a pulse beating his temple, and I thought, *poor devil*.

"You must tell us exactly what you want done. We're used to horses. Have you a bucket and a hay net, and where's his water trough?"

"Not so fast young lady," said the Hermit in his rusty voice. "You've not let me finish, have you? Your brother asked some pertinent questions which are waiting to be answered. Now then: the horse is called Caesar, on account of the nose; he's come from my sister who buys badly treated, misused, starving or ill animals and finds them good homes; and she thought it would do me good to have a horse in my field, which is going to waste, so she sent Caesar in a cattle truck without warning. She knew if she asked me first I would have said no. It's what you call in French a *fait accompli*." He paused then and coughed, "Chest all blocked up. Where was I?"

10

"Hay food," I said, liking the man for praising me.

"It's ordered, promised for today, best clover. He's not taking any exercise so he can do with clover; half a ton should see him through till May. He's a bit on the lean side, poor fellow."

"So what would you like us to do?" I asked.

The Hermit leaned against the rotten doorpost, which was pitted by woodworms tunnelling their way towards the light. The effort of talking to people seemed to have exhausted him for a moment; then he sighed and explained again that he could not go out because of his heart, so could we come every day to feed the horse for him? Or would that be too much to ask? The hay was in the barn, back of the house. He was a big horse, and, although the grass would soon be through, he would need close on half a bale a day.

Sophie said we should be absolutely delighted. The horse was fantastic, so beautifully kind and friendly. The Hermit said his sister, whom he had not seen in years, had had the cheek to send a saddle and bridle. Did she expect him to take up riding? He would fall off at once. He hadn't the strength to saw a log, let alone mount a horse. She should have shown more sense, after all she was coming up to sixty. He said he couldn't even walk down the garden path, and it was a crying shame, seeing he had been a rider once, a point-to-pointer, and quite a cricketer too, though you might not think it.

Presently we took our leave, saying we would be back that afternoon in case the hay had come. And so our friendship with the Hermit began, a friendship which we kept at first secret from our parents for fear that they might worry, believing the poor man to be mad, while we thought we knew the cause of his withdrawal into the ivy clad house and pitied him for his ill health and bad reputation and, without realising it, we began to stand up for

11

him when his name was mentioned. Many people were angry with him for allowing a beautiful old house to decay. There were villagers who said the Hermit should be shut away in an hospital or Special Home and others who said he should take a vow of poverty and silence and go into a monastery. But the Hermit had shut the door firmly in the faces of the busybodies. He had even turned his back on the vicar, and shouted rudely at a social worker knocking on his door. He only wanted to be left alone, to live and die, he said, in peace.

But Sophie and I cared to see him as no more than an invalid, because we wanted to look after his horse. We saw ourselves riding down the tracks that cut through the hop fields into the woods and down into the forests of nuts and oaks, which lie so thick in some of the Kentish valleys, where the wild rabbits lived and where at night the badgers left their setts to look for food under the light of the moon.

CHAPTER TWO

WHEN we met the Hermit our brother and sister, James and Julie, were aged eighteen months and three and a half years, and they kept our Mum very busy, especially James, who was still in nappies, suffered from eczema, asthma and all kinds of allergies and was, we thought (unfairly), very spoiled. His constant crying and demands for attention made Mum absentminded and so, although surprised that we had taken to cycling down the lane in early light before breakfast, she did not consider the question very deeply or make any objections.

We had to ride like the wind, for Sophie had to get back

in time to catch the school bus and I had a ten minute cycle ride to the secondary school in the next village to ours, and if I was even a minute late some beastly prefect would be sure to spot me and send me to the Headmaster and then I had to invent an excuse, for I couldn't tell him about Caesar because he was a secret. The Headmaster was a stickler for punctuality, which was, he had said on more than one occasion, the essence of good manners.

At first we never saw the Hermit at all and our hopes of riding gradually grew fainter and fainter. Then, one weekend, I climbed on Caesar's back from the top of the broken gate and straight away a window opened and out came the Hermit's head; and then we realised he had been watching us all the time.

"Careful how you go," he said. "Hold on, I'm coming down." He was wearing the same grey trousers and old pullover, and he seemed to have grown still thinner so that his cheek bones jutted out like little cliffs in his face and his fingers were mere twigs which could be snapped in two with the stamp of a foot.

Caesar, however, was fatter and he took me for a brisk walk right round the edge of the field, stopping now and then to nibble at the first green blades of grass which had pushed through the yellowing mat of last year's weeds.

When I arrived back at the gate, Sophie said, "My turn." But the Hermit said, "Hold on," darted back into the house and presently returned with the saddle and bridle.

"I should like to see you ride him," he said simply, and he stepped outside the house, just three steps, and held out the tack for Sophie to take.

"Me?" she asked.

"No, the boy first; he's the eldest and he's a better size for the horse."

I put the plaited reins over Caesar's head and he most obligingly opened his mouth to take the bit, but I could

13

not reach above his eyes to put the headpiece over his ears.

"Get astride the gate, then you'll reach," advised the Hermit, "and speak to Caesar. Let him hear your voice; he's trying to help, isn't he?"

From the gate I succeeded and then we saddled the horse. All the tack was old fashioned and expensive, made years ago before the war. The girth was folded leather—a Fitzwilliam, Sophie said, and the pelham was a Scamperdale, curved at the sides. We didn't know how to fix the curb chain and we put the girth round the wrong way, for we were only used to the nylon girths and egg-butt snaffles the Langtons owned. The Hermit, grimacing in the doorway, became impatient.

"Don't you know anything? Thought you were a horseman. Bit of a mutt, aren't you?" and then he took four steps to the little sagging gate which parted the garden from the field. He leaned over and pointed with his twig-like fingers.

"Twist the curb chain. Go on, until it's flat. Now pass it through the rings of the bit; that's how we did it in my day. *No*, that's too tight. Oh, bring the horse here!"

"Nincompoop!" hissed Sophie.

Presently the Hermit was actually leaning over the gate and giving us detailed instructions, and he showed no signs of falling down. He told us that the folded side of the girth must be nearest Caesar's elbows—that was common sense for then there would be no sharp edge to rub where the friction was. The saddle and bridle had belonged to him when he was a reckless young man.

"Now then," said the Hermit. "Let your sister give you a leg up. You have refused payment and it's only fair that you should have some reward for your work."

Caesar's stride was long and lively. After Mustard and Cress who were barely fourteen hands, he felt enormous and his ears seemed miles away. For a few minutes I was

14

a little nervous and the Hermit must have noted this for he said,

"Just walk him gently until you are used to him. There's no hurry. You've got all your life before you, bar bloody strife, war or accidents."

"You're a cheerful one!" said Sophie, in my mother's tone of voice when she is upbraiding the window cleaner, whose mind dwells on tragedy.

I was just about to trot Caesar when he threw up his head, snatching a little at his bit, as the clatter of hoofs on the road broke into the stillness of the afternoon like a shout at a concert, and the birds scattered.

"Hi!" cried Chris and Jane Langton. "What a surprise! In the Hermit's field. I say, what a fantastic horse. Isn't he smashing?"

In a flash the Hermit had dashed into the house and slammed the door.

"Idiots!" cried Sophie. "You've frightened him away!"

"Who, the old man? You talk as though he was a wild deer or something. But how come you have the use of his field and who owns the horse?"

Sophie started a long boring argument with the Langtons about the Hermit, whom they insulted in voices grown loud with the habit of shouting across fields at their farm. But I ignored them, for I wanted to seize the opportunity to enjoy a really long turn on Caesar. Soon I was trotting and then cantering him and I found that, in spite of his size, he was nimble and quite the most balanced and comfortable mount I had ridden.

The Langtons went to Sophie's school and so were more her friends than mine. Our parents approved of them because they were always polite to grown ups and never forgot to say "Thank you for having us", "What a fantastic cake. It's delicious", "Excuse me interrupting but . . ." and that sort of thing. But they could be spiteful and once in a moment of malice they had sneered at me for not passing the 11 plus; an exam which in those days qualified you for grammar school, and I never quite forgave them. Secretly I was friends with them only to please my mother and because occasionally they allowed me to ride their ponies. At that time I had no close friends, no teachers at school who inspired me to work and no special interest apart from animals and birds, which made the discovery of Caesar all the more important for me.

After a bit Jane shouted, "Give us a turn, Matthew." And I said no and she said I was being unfair, they let me ride *their* ponies. "Dog in the manger," she said. I retorted that Caesar wasn't mine to lend and Sophie said, "Perhaps, later." Then I looked up at the house and saw the Hermit watching from a bedroom window, and I realised that he had probably heard all the unkind things said about him, and I asked the Langtons to go, and, to my surprise, they went.

After they had gone the Hermit opened a window and called that Caesar was not to be ridden for more than forty minutes and only at the walk and trot, as he was out of condition. Sophie had a short turn and then we rubbed the horse down with old dry grass which we twisted into pads, poor imitations of the proper wisps made out of hay or straw by grooms. Then we returned the tack to the Hermit who came to the door when we banged on it.

"Those your friends, buddies?" he asked.

"Sophie's," I said.

"They are going to lend us the *Pony Club Manual of Horsemanship* so that we cope properly. They are all right really. They just got a little over-excited today," explained Sophie as though she was excusing the actions of a couple of terriers.

"So they think I'm a hermit or a religious fanatic. Romantic nonsense! Load of old rubbish. Malicious gossip," said

16

the Hermit. "I'm on my knees no more often than anyone else and if there's no God, what is life all about? There are others who say I'm a miser, miserable rotters! I know. I've heard it all from Perks who brings my groceries and bread. A great man, Perks, one of the old school. Ask him! I give him a fiver at Christmas, call him my supply line. But he keeps quiet about *that*, I'll be bound. "Don't they know an invalid when they see one? Now, listen, I'll get a bit extra, a bit of change from my Friday cheque from Perks, and on Saturday you can buy grooming tools for me and a bag of oats and some cubes or whatever they give horses nowadays. I expect everything has changed. If our friend Caesar is going to carry you around, he'll need a bit more to eat won't he?"

We said we would, and thank you and great, and how much we liked the horse; and then Sophie asked why the Hermit was frightened of the Langtons and for a moment he looked quite put out; his mouth twitched and he tugged at a bit of dirt on his grey sweater with one of his pale thin fingers. Then he cleared his throat and announced that he did not like being stared at.

"I don't really care for people any more," he added, avoiding our eyes. "Sounds silly but I've got used to you. You're all right, but, mark you, I won't even see my own sister. I'm as daft as that—to her disgust. That's why she sent the horse. She's at the end of her tether—she's been trying to bring me out for years. She knows my weakness for horses. It's the Irish in me; it's innate, bred in the bone. And she wants to take me out of myself."

"But your heart?" said Sophie.

"Oh yes, my heart," said the Hermit, "rotten old heart."

I was a little annoyed with Sophie for embarrassing the Hermit and I didn't want to remember the way his mouth had twitched.

17

"You shouldn't have asked," I told her, as we mounted our cycles. "You were tactless."

"I wanted to know."

"You made him admit he was frightened, and that must be a hard thing for a grown-up to do, especially to children."

"He said he was daft, did you hear?"

"Well, he's not. He's just an invalid."

In spite of my denial we suddenly wondered whether our parents might be right and the Hermit might be truly mad. He might seize us, drag us indoors, tie us to chairs and kill us with a carving knife and bury us in the copse with the woodpeckers tapping our funeral dirge. We let our imaginations run away with us as our feet pedalled faster and faster and the sharp March wind whipped our cheeks a rosy apple red. We were almost sick with fear and then, remembering how feeble the poor man was, how frail his face, thinking of Caesar's welcoming whinny each morning we calmed down again. We did not want to believe that the Hermit was insane, for if we did there would be no more riding, no more visits to the ivy-clad house and the field which we had begun to think of as our own. Eventually, slowing down, talking it over, letting our wildest thoughts run riot aloud, we purged ourselves of fear.

"Anyway, one out of ten people in Britain is likely to go mad at least once in her life time," said Sophie in a worldly way.

"How do you know?"

"Heard it on T.V."

But the secret was out. The Langtons had talked, and the lady in the village shop warned us not to go down to see the old miser in the lane:

"Got a horse, has he?" she said handing us each a packet of sherbert. "He's a poor old man to be sure, but not to be trusted. A bit weak in the head, they say. And

18

there's always a first time. They say he's harmless, but you never know. He lives on powdered milk, they say. Dreadful what these strange men do to children sometimes."

"He's not strong enough to hurt a fly," I said.

"Ah, that's what *you* think. He's money down there, so they say, and strange habits."

But in our minds we had lived through the worst and so we dismissed the old lady's warning, while wondering who "they" might be. The next day we slipped off into town on our cycles, while James was in one of his states and our Mum distracted, and bought grooming tackle: body and dandy brushes, curry comb and stable rubber and a nice steel hoof pick. And that was all Sophie's money from her last birthday spent, but we believed again in the Hermit's sanity and honesty and we were sure he would pay us back.

It was mid-March now, windy and bright with little clouds skidding across blue skies like tiny motor boats in a lake. The Hermit's garden was busy with nesting birds, for spring had come early. Housemartins were already building nests of mud under the eaves of the house; the woodpeckers had redoubled their tapping, and a pair of robins had woven a nest in a kettle on a shelf in the barn where Caesar's hay was stored. In the ivy, too, many little nurseries were under construction, and thrushes and sparrows darted joyfully in and out of the thorn hedges which were just breaking into verdant leaf. If only, I thought, we had a decent biology teacher at school, someone who really cared for natural history, instead of keeping us in the lab day in day out, what a fabulous time we could have down here working on a project! I imagined myself taking photographs, making notes, winning the Natural History prize of the year. Only at our school there were no prizes, simply grading and streaming; the biology

19

teacher was as old as the hills, turning deaf, and disagreeable. He liked the boys who were good at maths, because they could work out statistics and were useful in biological experiments, and he disliked the countryside, ditches, scrub and ponds (partly, I suspect, because he was too clumsy or too old to scramble through undergrowth or stand knee-deep in water). Father said matters would improve when Sophie's school became a sixth form college and mine a comprehensive school.

"You'll get a better class of teacher, then," he insisted. But meanwhile we all thought we were the ones who got second best because we were not clever enough to win a place at the grammar school, and that made us resentful —or I think it did. And some times this resentment even followed me down to the enchantment of the Hermit's garden and made me angry as I watched the birds or listened to Sophie's stories of the grammar school, where the biology teacher was a young woman deeply interested in insects.

Miraculously, in spite of the Langtons' chatter, no one told our parents of our visits to the Hermit's field, although many people were now talking about the horse which had arrived in a cattle truck to live there, and more than one person announced that she had seen the Hermit's head peeping through an open window. Our Mum, overworked, anxious and housebound, allowed us to go almost anywhere so long as we remained together. She had long ago graded us in her own special way, deciding that I was slow but sensible, the practical one, whereas Sophie was quick minded but flighty. We made a pretty reliable pair, she said, and being a trained infant teacher, she felt she knew how to assess children, even her own.

"Matthew always looks before he leaps," she would announce to other mothers. "He's cautious. Heaven help us if he doesn't get any O levels. Oh well, I suppose he can always be a furniture restorer—lots of money in that—or go into the paper mill like his Dad."

But sometimes she wasn't so philosophical about my future. When she was tired, when James had broken her night's sleep with his itching or want of breath, she would nag me about my poor work at school. "You'll never get to university at this rate. You'll have to be a dustman," she would say, and her words were like a chain around my neck; they were the dead weight of failure.

The day after we bought the grooming tools the Hermit gave us a letter to post, addressed to the local corn merchant, for he realised that we had forgotten all about the oats and cubes.

"I may not mix much, but, mark you, I still write letters. I'm in touch with the world even if I don't appear to be in it . . ." He gave a sort of cackle which was a poor imitation of a laugh. I believe he had not laughed for so long that he had forgotten how to do it.

He paid us for the grooming tools.

"You've done well. You've got sense—I like that." He was leaning against his door post. "You know I had a mare once called Skylark, dappled grey like a rocking horse, pretty as a picture, but couldn't stand the body brush, ticklish, kicked and squealed every time you ran it over her ribs. But a corker to ride, a real corker. And game! She would turn her head at nothing, a super jumper."

"Fabulous!" said Sophie, "I love greys. I love their mushroom noses and dark eyes."

"You use the word love too loosely," objected the Hermit. "You mean you *like* greys; you admire them, yes?"

"I suppose so," said Sophie, a little crestfallen.

"I have a snapshot of her somewhere which I'll show you one of these days. My wife liked that horse, too. Like you, she had a weakness for greys."

21

"You were married?" Sophie's eyes grew large. She could not see him in the role of husband.

"Oh yes, yes, I was married once, before the war. Centuries ago, centuries—or so it seems now. Sometimes at night I try to remember her face, to recall her changes of expression; the way she smiled—the sort of things photos don't really convey, and I can't. It's uncanny. And then sometimes, it will all come back to me in a flash; it is almost as though she is beside me. She was quite a horsewoman, I can tell you. We both used to ride in point-to-points. She won a couple of Ladies Races," he paused for a moment while we stared at him with open mouths, trying to understand this new Hermit. "You wouldn't think it would you? Not now, seeing me now that I can't walk beyond my front door. But believe me, I was quite a dashing young man once—in the old days, just before the war. You think I'm kidding?" A curtain of sadness came across his face; the warmth in his eyes faded like a little fire deprived suddenly of the bellows and, bewildered, we said,

"Yes."

"No."

And then,

"Maybe."

And,

"Yes, of course. We always thought you were."

And vainly we tried to picture the bent pathetic wreck of a man straight and strong with suntanned arms and legs which sent him springing into the saddle on his lively grey mare.

Then, wanting to change the subject, Sophie said:

"When a steeplechaser or point-to-pointer jumps he puts in a short stride just before take-off, while a showjumper puts in a long stride—is that right?"

"Absolutely, more or less. Either of you hungry? I've got a packet of biscuits inside, scrumptious biscuits, wheatmeal chocolate, used to love those when I was a kid."

We looked at one another; our parents' fears uppermost in our minds. The Hermit took a step sideways making room for us to precede him into the house. He looked like a ghost, so white and fragile that we would not have been surprised at that moment if he had dissolved into thin air.

"Not today, thank you," I said, like a housewife turning away a door-to-door salesman, stiff with embarrassment and saddled with a guilty feeling that we were letting down our friend by suspecting that his motives were mixed.

"It's fantastically kind of you," added Sophie, overdoing things a bit.

"Just as you please," said the Hermit. "Goodbye then." He closed the door.

"We've hurt his feelings," said Sophie.

"Yes, but he'll get over it. I mean grown-ups don't bother too much about children—I mean what children do socially."

"Who would have thought he was married?"

"I don't see why not, in his young days. Everyone is young at some time or other. It stands to reason."

Every evening now we rode Caesar after school and each time he seemed to become easier and more obliging, which probably meant we were riding better and he found us easier to understand. He was too large for us, but we found an old tea chest in the barn which we used as a mounting block, until one day the top caved in and I sat down hard on my behind, right on a thistle which made Sophie collapse in a fit of giggles. We also found six rusty petrol tins which we used to mark out a school, and we borrowed our Dad's grass hook, and I cut down all the tall yellowing grass so that the young spring blades could come through, but we left the undergrowth for the animals, birds and insects who made it their home.

One day after cantering round the school slowly on the correct leg, I called to the Hermit, who was standing at his door as usual, to ask the horse's age.

"Look and see," he said, shifting his weight from one leg to the other.

So I dismounted and peered into Caesar's mouth, which I prised open by pressing my fingers on the bars.

"How?"

"Well, is he long in the tooth?"

"Long in the tooth?"

"Yes, have his gums receded, do his teeth look long?"

"I don't know; I've never looked in a horse's mouth before."

"Has he black hollows on the tables of his teeth?"

"How do you mean?"

"Oh, bring him here, boy!" cried the Hermit in a moment of exasperation, and, forgetting about our resolve to keep our friend at arm's length, I led Caesar to the gate. Forgetting all about his dicky heart, the Hermit came to the gate, leaned over and opened Caesar's mouth.

"About ten," he said.

I noticed then that the Hermit's eyes had lost their paleness, the dead, faraway look; they had come alive and his ivory cheeks glowed faintly pink.

"Ride him round once again. I want to see you canter him straight from a walk," he said, seeming for the moment quite an ordinary man, not strange at all, "Come on, put a bit more energy in it! Get down in the saddle."

Sophie who had been searching the barn for a pole to use as a jump came back and claimed her turn, but the Hermit said no, wait until the lad had cantered from a walk.

Sophie, who is incurably curious about human nature, then went up to the Hermit, almost touched him on the shoulder and asked whether he had children of his own.

24

Bending forward, looking up into the man's face, she seemed like a piece of china. Her nose could well have belonged to one of those porcelain shepherdesses people used to put on their chimney pieces. The Hermit smiled— yes, his lips actually stretched right across his face like pieces of elastic; and then a dreadful look of sadness blotted out the smile; he turned away as though he could not bear to meet Sophie's enquiring gaze and for me his answer was drowned in a gust of wind which sent the old trees creaking and the hedges quivering.

On the way home Sophie told me that the Hermit had said he had had a boy who was dead and buried along with his mother, poor lad. And then, ridiculously, we frightened ourselves again by wondering whether he had murdered them, and whether he might murder us and bury us in the nettles at the back of the house by the cesspit.

Mum was at our garden gate when we reached home, her fair hair all pulled and tangled by the wind and her cheeks bright with anxiety. She is small and slight, with a sharp determined chin and eyes which show her feelings.

"How could you?" she asked. "How could you do it?"

"Do what?" we chorused, although in our hearts we knew her meaning.

We dismounted from our cycles, threw them down carelessly in the grass.

"Chris came with that Pony Club book. Haven't I warned you about talking to strange men?"

"Strange men?" We were playing for time.

"The man down the lane, the recluse. You know who I mean. Now don't play dumb. I can't bear it!"

I thought then of Caesar; his noble head, his soft nose, the feel of his powerful stride as I cantered him in the field. I thought how he had changed our lives, making the coming of another day a special joy because there was something special to do.

"He isn't strange," I shouted. "He's just a bit of a hermit. He's tired of the world, the noise and all that . . ."

"He's mad," said Mum. "He never goes out because he's mad. And now he's tempted you around to his place with a horse, cunning, very cunning."

"He's all right," said Sophie, "honestly Mum."

"Never!"

My heart started to hammer and my glasses tipped forward; she had a fixed idea of the man; she had labelled him. It wasn't fair.

"We went there when we saw Caesar. You know we like horses. He didn't invite us. He didn't want the horse, as a matter of fact. His sister sent him, see. She thought he was lonely and she knows he loves—well *likes*—horses. He was a great point-to-pointer once. Where's your evidence? If he's mad, prove it!" My voice was loud.

"That's not the way to speak to me," said Mum. "And don't shout. Now apologise."

I said I was sorry, of course, and then Sophie put her hand on our Mum's arm. "Don't take on," she said. "Don't upset yourself."

They were the very words our Mum had used to calm us in the old days when we came back from school in a state about some lesson which had gone wrong. I pushed my glasses back to the bridge of my nose.

"Don't stop us going," I pleaded.

"His wife and son are dead. You should be sorry for him," added Sophie, and then she put on a very prim voice and said, "The whole village should be ashamed for being so uncharitable. Mad indeed! Cheek! The poor man has a weak heart; he can't work; he's an invalid."

"And how did his wife and son die?" asked our Mum.

"I don't know, of some disease or other, a fire or something, I suppose."

"He's no stronger than a blade of grass, honestly a puff

of wind would knock him over. I don't know what you're fussing about."

Then James started to cry and fair-haired Julie, who looks like an advertisement for magarine, came running out of the house with an open pot of unwashable ink in her hand, a black trail following in her wake; and all was commotion. When our little brother and sister were clean, tidy and quiet Mum told us she would discuss the Hermit again when Dad came home.

Dad was calmer; he is a big man heavily built, but very upright, and slow of speech. Sometimes he seems like a rock behind which you can shelter when a storm rises. He sat down in the deep yellow armchair and said:

"Now then, you two, let's get things straight. This man, this recluse, has a horse which needs care and attention, which he can't supply because of his heart, so he's enlisted the help of you kids—right?"

"Right," we echoed feeling more hopeful.

"But the man keeps himself to himself, never goes out, so he might be mad, but we've no evidence against him. Shall I go to see him?"

"No, please *don't*," said Sophie. "Please Dad. Something terrible has happened, had made him frightened of people. He's like a nervous animal and he's just getting accustomed to us. It isn't only his heart."

"He's weak as water. We could push him over; he's like a cardboard man; it's hard to think that he is made of skin and bone and muscle."

"He's mental, not right up top, got a screw loose?" suggested Dad, shifting in the chair, then scratching his nose.

"He seems to manage his life, groceries are delivered along with bread and things every Friday. He cashes cheques, writes letters. Look, we never go into the house.

We are not that silly. Anyway the two of us are more than a match for him."

"He's just a sick, kind, lonely old man," said Sophie in a worldly sort of way.

"I'm going to ring the police," said Dad springing from his chair. "*That's* what I'm going to do. They'll know if he's a kinky sort of bloke."

"Why, you're not going to have him arrested? He's done nothing wrong, just let us ride Caesar and given us a bit of instruction," I cried. "Listen, Dad, we love going down there. It means a lot to us. We've been feeding the horse for several weeks now. It's a bit late to start fussing. We must do *something*. You never take us anywhere. We get so bored. Day after day just the same . . . It's not fair. Everything is arranged for James and Julie, not us, so we've made our own arrangements. Get lost, Dad!"

I had not meant to say so much, but my tongue had run away with me so that the words seemed to come unbidden from my mouth.

"That's not the way to speak to your father. Quieten down or go to your room. I'm boss here," said Dad. "Now then, I'm ringing the police for your own protection and good. I don't want the man arrested. If everything is above board he won't be, will he? It stands to reason. If he has a record . . ."

"What's a record?" I asked miserably.

"A record of some crime."

"Caesar's the best thing that has ever happened in our whole life. It's like having an animal of our own. It would be different if I was a soccer player or a swimmer or something, but you hardly ever take us anywhere, and now we've got our riding; it's great Dad, don't you see?"

"Fantastic," said Sophie.

"All right, all right, point taken," said Dad. "Now both

quieten down. Your mother's tired, have a thought for her and keep your voices down. Right?"

"Right," we agreed.

He went away to telephone just the same, while we waited with bated breath, but returned almost at once, saying the police would phone him back. The man at the station seemed a bit of a nit-wit.

We watched the last part of children's hour on television and Sophie and I played with James and Julie who were really very sweet when well, if you were in the mood for babies. Mum hung out nappies on the line.

"Time he was dry," she muttered.

Then she toasted crumpets which we ate after sausages and mash, washed down with cups of milk or tea.

The police rang back at a quarter to seven. James was in his bath, but Sophie, Julie and I stood by Dad trying to overhear the conversation. Julie, who is jealous of the telephone, vigorously shook a rattle in the hope of turning Dad's attention back to herself. Suddenly he lost his temper, put down the phone and drove us all away. We stood in the passage biting our finger nails. Or rather *I* bit my nails and Sophie fiddled with the zips on her track suit.

But Dad was angry with us, even after he had put down the receiver.

"Why must you *always* make a noise when I'm on the 'phone?" he asked in tones of extreme exasperation. "You do it every darned time; it's deliberate. Matthew, you're old enough to know better, soon be fourteen. I started work when I was fourteen, earned my living. Sophie, why did you allow Julie to shake that rattle? You are not toddlers now you know. Have you no common sense?"

"Can we still go?" I asked, instead of apologising which would have been the polite and tactful thing to do.

"Wait and see," said Dad.

29

"He's all right, isn't he?"

Grown-ups can be very irritating. They do not see how minutes can seem to children like hours. Of course waiting made us bad tempered and I pushed Julie when she kept bothering me to play "grandmother steps" or "What's the time, Mr. Wolf?" and she slipped and fell. Unhurt she still yelled, then told our Mum that I was bad and rough, so that I was sent upstairs with five pence docked from next week's pocket money.

"Little sneak," I muttered, but she would not have understood.

"Big boys mustn't bully little girls. I'm surprised at your behaviour," called Mum.

I lay on my bed and started *Swallows and Amazons*, by Arthur Ransome, but soon threw it down in disgust because I could not stand the children; they were so obedient. I could not imagine Sophie obeying me as Mate Susan and Titty obeyed their bossy brother, John, who was Captain. Perhaps I was jealous of John, so secure in his superior position as eldest in a family of four. He never, I noted, picking up the book again and skimming through it, pushed the younger ones; he just gave them the more boring jobs to do and they did them.

At last bedtime came and when my mother came to bid me goodnight, she said we could still go to see the Hermit, but we must not go alone and it would be wiser not to enter the house.

"The police have nothing against him, and nothing for him either, if it comes to that. But he has no criminal record, and they believe him to be simply a harmless eccentric old man. There's a Mr. Perks from the grocers farther down the valley who keeps an eye on him and delivers meat, veg, etc. He knows about the horse and about you two feeding it."

I said, "Great" and Sophie, who came in then in her

quilted dressing gown, said, "Fabulous," which was predictable. And our Mum said she wished that we would widen our vocabularly, and would I go back to the bathroom and wash my feet again? They looked filthy and I would smell. Then Dad came upstairs with his heavy purposeful tread. He stood in the bedroom and, raising his eyebrows, which are bushy like those adorning the face of a prominent trade union leader who often appears on television, said if the horse interfered with our homework or school work that would be the end of our riding. Without education we would be lost in today's world, and I had to look ahead to O levels and pull myself out of the rut which had graded me C. We were coming into the technological age, said Dad, where brains would be needed more than brawn. If I worked I could easily become a B child. It was simply a case of applying myself.

Knowing that he thought my figure too weedy, I told him that riding would make me fit, and a fit body made a lively brain; I would learn to straighten my back. Sophie showed him a picture of a good seat in the Pony Club Manual.

"Well, it might make a man of you," Dad said, and, although his words were not altogether kind, I had the impression that he was rather pleased that we had spunk enough to take up riding on so large a horse. But I was still cross with him for withholding the information he had gained from the police for playing, as I saw it, cat and mouse with our dreams and hopes. And, after scrubbing my feet I went to sleep, half pleased and half angry, to dream that Dad came down to the Hermit's house to watch us ride, but, once I was mounted he donned a policeman's helmet, arrested our frail friend and drove him off handcuffed to Sophie in a panda car.

I woke sweating in the middle of the night to see a silver moon sailing like a queen across a glassy sky.

CHAPTER THREE

THE next day we went down to the field in the blue light of early evening, our pockets full of sugar. Caesar whinnied to us, his eyes dark and friendly, his neat ears pricked. As he came across the field briskly with his long, sweeping stride to nuzzle in our pockets, we, who had never before possessed a living thing, were suddenly filled with unforgettable happiness. Big and fine and beautiful, he looked down on us as his friends, smelling of damp grass, of the wet trees which now stood so still against the steely horizon. Above us a solitary crow rose like a black plane into the twilight flapping black wings, while at our feet the first spring blades of grass were pushing through into the light bringing green to mingle with the muted shades of last year's growth.

In silence we fetched the saddle and bridle, brushed the mud from the horse's back and legs, tacked him up; and then searched in vain for the Hermit, using our voices now to call his name, banging the old knocker on the rotten door and tapping on the window panes.

"Perhaps he's dead," I said.

"He's hiding. He's in one of his unsociable moods," suggested Sophie in a voice of awe.

"Let's go out on the road. He won't mind, and if he's dead he won't know."

"You're being mean."

"I'm not!"

All at once I felt quite devilish and full of bravado. School had been boring, the biology teacher, whom I considered incompetent, a drag, but I had kept my thoughts

32

and moods in check. Now they bubbled over in callous recklessness.

"We can't help it if the old boy's dead."

I regretted my words as soon as they left my lips, but I wasn't going to let Sophie know that.

"He might be ill."

"Oh, come on! Bags ride first."

I mounted at once before she could object.

"We shall get caught in the dark. We have no lights on our cycles."

Her voice was a wail like the threat of the sea when you are safe on land. And if there is arrogance in your soul the stride of a good horse under you may increase it.

"Oh, boo-boo!" I cried, and then I quoted, rolling out the words:

"Away! the moor is dark beneath the moon,
 Rapid clouds have drank the last pale beam of even:
 Away! the gathering winds will call the darkness soon
 And profoundest midnight shroud the serene lights of
     heaven."

"I thought you didn't like poetry," said Sophie, catching up on her cycle.

"We learned that today—Shelley."

"Yes, I know."

It was lovely to be so high, to see over the hedges right into the cottage gardens, to feel the frosty air sharp against my cheeks, borne along as I was by that great sweeping stride, eating up yards and miles. I sang and, cycling beside me, Sophie sang, too, and from a bare tree a blackbird's haunting notes drifted across the landscape and was lost in the wooded hills.

It was a night for the wildest dreams, for building castles in the air, for letting your voice ring out across the dusky fields, for riding over the hills and far away. Have you ever been intoxicated by such a night? We saw ourselves winning point-to-points, leading the way in the hunting field. We saw our smiling faces in the newspapers, our happy hands holding silver-plated cups. And while our fantasies grew the blue light turned to grey as dusk's cloak fell carelessly across the brown shouldered woods and then the sleeping fields, the high banked lanes and all the little cottages. And on their perches in branch or hedge the birds fell silent and closed their eyes for sleep.

"My turn," wailed Sophie. "Don't be mean. Come on!" But the devil was with me still.

"'Tisn't," I said.

"'Tis!"

"All . . ." I meant to say All right. Come on then. I meant to be decent and fair at last, to dismount and hand the horse to her in brotherly fashion, to be nice. But before I finished my sentence I was jerked forward in the saddle; the long neck, the pricked ears went down before me, the stoney lane came up to meet me; the dust was gritty in my mouth, the flints harsh against my chin. Then I was separated from Caesar altogether. He stood up again, and, after a moment, I found myself on my knees, a little warm blood trickling down my chin. The world was straight again with the dark sky above me and the ground beneath taking my weight.

"Are you all right? His leg is bleeding. Oh look, Matthew, his knee! Oh goodness, what is the Hermit going to say?"

I stood up, spat out the grit, wiped the dust and blood from my face, felt the dizziness in my head subside. Then I focussed my attention on Caesar who stood now dejectedly, head down, sides heaving.

"It's not a bad cut, is it?"

We peered in the gathering dusk.

"It's dark blood, which means it isn't a artery, but it's

34

on a joint, and that's bad I suppose. Oh curse and damn!"
My head was starting to spin and somewhere in my brain
a pair of hot tongs seemed to be pinching me.

"We must lead him back and tell the Hermit. Come on,
it's getting dark. Take my bike."

Sophie was in command. I followed her instructions,
diminished by the thought that I might be to blame for the
accident. Dimly I remembered that when Black Beauty
fell, the rider was blamed and that a wounded knee was
a calamity.

"We shall need a vet. We should have asked the Hermit's permission before taking him on the road, specially
as he has no shoes. I told you so, didn't I? But you
wouldn't listen!"

"And it's all my fault. Go on, say it! Rub it in!" I
cried, tasting blood in my mouth from a cut on my lip.
"Just now I wish I was dead."

Darkness was coming down quickly; the distance
between us and the nearest tree was growing shorter and
shorter until visibility was down to feet rather than yards.
And now the owl's cry had replaced the blackbird's song
and the eyes of cats shone in the darkness like marbles of
silver fire. There was a deep stillness in the lanes, an eeri-
ness which made us drop our voices and move closer to
one another; yet here and there the warm glow of lights,
muffled by curtains, reminded us of human life at hand.
At last we saw one light shining from the Hermit's house,
the solid outline of his roof and the wedge of a chimney
stack against the ink black sky. I felt for a minute as
though I had been through a mangle, as though all the
courage and strength has been squeezed out of me into the
bucket below. Then coming into the golden glow of light,
seeing the Hermit's anxious figure, white and ghost-like on
the doorstep, I felt a rush of energy.

"We've done a terrible thing," I said. "We've taken out

Caesar without asking you and we've let him—I've let him—fall down in the lane."

"Are his knees broken?"

"Broken—the bones?" asked Sophie, her voice a little shrill in the heavy darkness of the night.

"No, the skin, you mutt!"

"Yes, it's bleeding," said Sophie.

"It's only one knee," I added.

"Bring him into the light. I can't come out. I shall fall down, my palpitations!"

It took a few moments to persuade Caesar to go up to the door and when he did, he gave the Hermit such a butt with his nose that the poor man spun backwards like some scarecrow tumbled by a sudden gust of wind.

He straightened himself again, looking flustered, then inspected the wound.

"It's got some grit in it. Can't leave dirt in a wound. Hold on, I'll fetch a bowl of salt and water."

"Salt will sting," said Sophie. "He'll never let us ride Caesar again, and I don't blame him. It's all over, Matthew. It's finished—our visits here and everything."

"Oh for goodness sake, dry up!"

"It's your fault. I said not to take him out."

"You came."

"Only against my better judgement. Only because you simply rode off!"

"Please will you shut up or I shall explode."

My lip was hurting now, my head spinning, the tongs little forks of fire, and my conscience was pricking me like a thousand thorns. I felt I had let everyone down, that I was what Dad would call a heel, but I wasn't going to admit that, least of all to my young sister.

The Hermit came back with a chipped enamel bowl and a wedge of yellowing cotton wool.

"Steady there, whoa, hold him still; Speak to him!

Come on, let's have a bit of horse sense for a change! Nice soothing voices, that's better!"

The horse kept backing away and throwing up his head; his eyes rolled back and we saw his whites, and his hoofs scraped on the cobbled path.

"Whoa, my little lovely, come on, my beauty. There's a fine fellow, there, there." The Hermit spoke like an experienced and kind-hearted blacksmith shoeing a horse, and every now and then he paused in his work to pat Caesar on the neck.

"Lockjaw," he muttered, as he bathed out the last speck of grit. "Always a danger with this sort of cut. The vets have something for it now, so my sister told me, an injection, came in after the war," he was muttering almost to himself but we hung on his words scenting danger.

"There, that'll do."

The Hermit had finished. "Now I'll get a bandage," he said, "I've a supply of first aid equipment upstairs. I went through a fearful phase and Mr. Perks bought me it—to set my mind at rest, seeing I'm so cut-off from doctors. Oh dear me, I imagined all sorts of things for a week or two and then I was all right, the ogres subsided and I saw daylight again."

Presently the wound was neatly bound, first in lint, then in a cotton bandage followed by a crepe bandage.

"Now put him in the field with an armful of hay and ring the vet as soon as you can. I don't know who he is or where he is. But you can find out. Tell him the horse needs protection against lockjaw—or call it tetanus if you want to sound more knowledgeable."

Without lights on our cycles, we rode back very cautiously, listening all the time for approaching cars, so that we could retreat from them into the ditch or, where space allowed, on to the verge, but silence reigned and not a vehicle appeared. As we came to the hump-backed bridge, the clouds parted showing us the moon hanging like some pale disc cut by man to decorate a backcloth of velvet. It was strange and beautiful but our hearts were heavy and we were in no mood to enjoy the loveliness of an English night.

We came home with hardly a word between us and, back in our house, we told Mum that Caesar had slipped and fallen on the road and we must ring the vet, whoever he might be, without delay. We tried to play down the accident, but my mother saw my swollen lip and cut chin and dragged me to the bathroom, so that she too could remove the grit and inspect the wounds. They were little more than grazes and she was soon satisfied. She told us the vet's name was Sizer—she knew because the neighbour often took her cat for treatment for his eczema—and then she returned to cooking the supper without noticing that we had cycled back in the dark without lights. Our Mum is so busy that, out of sheer self-protection, she shuts her eyes to many of our actions in which I believe other mothers would have found cause for rebuke. She hates arguments because they upset her and with so much work on her hands she cannot afford to be upset. Sometimes when I looked at our Mum I used to vow that if I married I would plan for only two children. More in my opinion meant slavery.

Mr. Sizer was brisk and business-like. He said he would be along about nine in the morning. His abrupt tone made me apprehensive and I feared he would tell me off for riding Caesar on the road without shoes. I remembered that when Black Beauty fell he was missing a shoe. I saw Mr. Sizer in my mind's eye as a small, fierce, sandy-haired man with a bristling moustache the colour of shredded wheat. He would dress in cord trousers and checked coat with the sort of handwoven tie you find in the Lake District. His hair, I decided, would be neat and short, with a

38

wave on the top, and in common with my biology master, he would take an exception to mine which I wore down to the level of my chin.

When I told my mother that I must take the morning off school to prevent Caesar dying from lockjaw she raised no objections.

"I suppose it could come under 'rural studies'. Isn't that the in-thing nowadays? I mean dealing with vets and things, all amongst the birds and the beasts," she suggested mildly. "It's educational in the broader sense."

"Absolutely," I said and I was so pleased with her response that I threw my arms round her neck and kissed her on both cheeks.

Perhaps, I reflected, tomorrow would be a better day; perhaps all would be well in the end, and the knee would mend without a scar. Joint oil came into my dreams; dark and thick as motor oil, it spilled down Caesar's legs—both knees were broken in this dream—and the Hermit stood by wringing his hands, in a nightgown and with a cap on his head like Uncle Ebeneezer in Stevenson's book, *Kidnapped*. And I was bowed down by guilt. Oh yes, the guilt was heavy on my back and shoulders, like a sack of coal; it was a dead weight under which my legs quaked and my heart grew sore. It was this weight which seemed to stay with me when I wakened, causing the cornflakes at breakfast to taste sodden and stale and the milk like whitewash.

"For heaven's sake, don't look so glum!" cried our Mother. "The world hasn't come to an end because the horse has a cut knee."

"Supposing he's lost joint oil?"

"Then he'll have a stiff joint," said Mum.

"He won't be rideable any more."

"No, I suppose not. Now, for heaven's sake, stop picking over those cornflakes and eat properly."

39

"It would be terrible if he died," said Sophie, who was without mercy this morning. "You would feel awful all your life, then."

"Now don't be melodramatic, that's one of your besetting sins," said our Mum.

"I'm not. I'm just looking facts in the face. Can I have some weetabix and is the soft brown sugar finished?"

"Look and see," said Mum, turning her attention to James.

It started to rain from a dull sky without a glimmer of white or blue to break the monotony. In the garden the shut crocuses bowed their heads; the bare wintry trees dripped and tiny petals fell, bright as amber, from the tall forsythia by the brick garage.

The guilt and apprehension had not gone, unlike the little tongs of fire which had been drowned in sleep, and I felt near tears.

"Coffee, do you think dear, kind Mum, that I might have a little this morning? My head is thick, my brain wrapped in cotton wool."

"At your age? It's a drug, you know. And you mustn't rely on drugs every time you have a bit of bad news."

It was one of our mother's fads that children and young people should not drink coffee, which she insisted was a stimulant to which you could become addicted. In her defence I must say that one of her friends once drank so much black coffee that the whites of her eyes yellowed and she suffered a liver complaint. Usually Sophie and I only drank coffee secretly in cafes, like forbidden fruit, much to the surprise of our friends.

"It won't become a habit, I promise."

"All right, if you put plenty of milk in. Hurry, Sophie, or you'll miss the bus."

The rain was teeming down when I mounted my cycle, the lane turning into a river and the trees tossing like broken sails in a vicious wind. The air was sharp and cold against my face with that special English dampness which seems to reach the very marrow of your bones. The lane was deserted; the hump-backed bridge empty save for a forlorn wood pigeon waiting on the wall.

When I reached the field a bedraggled Caesar was standing, resting a leg, under the elder tree, his forelock plastered down with rain, his eyes dreamy as though he were looking back to foalhood. He whinnied faintly when he saw me, without pricking his ears or moving an inch. He was, I thought, the very picture of dejection. Was his jaw already locked, his spine stiffened with the advance of the dread disease? I wanted to cry; my heart seemed to thump madly in its cage of ribs and I felt a little sweat dripping coldly down my body. But it was no good standing around despondently. For the time being I must put a good face on the whole sorry affair.

I fetched the headcollar from the barn, splashed through the puddles to the elder tree.

"Come on, what's up?" I asked in my heartiest tone. "Feeling a bit depressed?"

I fished a lump of sugar from my pocket and watched him savour it, then push me with his soft muzzle for another. The rain was dark on his flanks; the bandage had slipped, revealing the wound, clotted with blood but clean, in a knee twice its normal size.

"Lost any oil, stiff, are you?"

Oh, I felt awful! I can't tell you how awful! I was talking mainly to keep up my spirits, but of course Caesar made no answer. He merely stood quite still in the rain with the patient look of an over-worked ox. For a moment it seemed like the end of all our hopes and fantasies.

I was urging Caesar to walk when the vet turned up in a *Range-Rover*, a cheery plump man with pink, wind-chafed cheeks and a scant, fair beard. Wearing stout wel-

41

lington boots over corduroy trousers and a riding mackintosh, he came across the field, a smile of welcome on his face.

"What a day. So this is the patient. Nice looking horse. Can we take him inside somewhere? A bit stiff, is he? Nasty old knee. Come along, old fellow, walk on, that's the way."

"He's miserable," I said. "He won't even prick his ears."

"So would you be with a cut like that on your knee. Come on, keep going. Just walk beside him, that's right, jolly good. Well done!"

"Do you think he's lost any joint oil?"

"Can't tell till I've examined him."

We took Caesar into the barn, which smelt deliciously of hay.

"And now water, cotton wool and a bowl."

The Hermit had put them all ready in his back porch, with a little note, saying "The vet will need these" and another note saying, "Please do not disturb me."

The vet cleaned the wound, dressed it with anti-biotic ointment and bandaged it with cotton wool, lint and elastoplast. Then he gave Caesar two injections, one anti-tetanus and one long term anti-biotic.

"He'll have a scar of course, but he's not a show horse, is he, so not to worry. The knee won't be weakened in any way. How did it happen?"

"My fault. I suppose I wasn't attending. I was arguing with my sister."

"Tut, tut. You can't always prevent a fall, but next time you take him out keep him up to the bit. Do you know what I mean?"

"Impulsion and all that."

"Nudge him along with your legs, so that you can feel

him at the other end of the rein saying 'Okay, I'm here, what's the next order'."

"I'll try," I said. "I'm quite a beginner, really."

"Keep him in this barn. Its ideal. He can move about, so he won't get too stiff. But fence off that hay or he'll mess it up. You know what horses are. Wasteful devils —they take no thought for the morrow."

"When do you think we can ride him again?"

"Ah, good question," replied the vet, chewing a stalk of straw flattened by a baler on the harvest field. "When he's sound, about a couple of weeks, I should think. He should go on all right. Give me a ring if things go wrong."

"And what do we do?"

"Change the bandage every three days, cut it off squeezing in this," he waved the tube of anti-biotic at me, "exactly as you saw me do it. Right? Push the nozzle right in in under the flap of skin. All right?"

"The bandage?"

"I'll leave the rest of this one with you. Should last another three times and, after that nothing. Right?"

"Right."

"Now, who do I send the account to? You or the old man?"

"Better send it to me. I may pass it on, but it was my fault, you see."

"I shouldn't be too gloomy about that. Accidents *do* happen, even when the best precautions are taken and it's impossible usually to allot the blame."

"Funny old set-up this," he went on a moment later, pausing on his way to the car to look up at the house. "A bit queer in the head, is he?"

"No, not at all. Just a hermit, no more. He prefers to live alone, contracted out, I suppose you could say—a bit of a hedgehog. I don't see why people shouldn't retire from the world if they want to—I mean lots of people

43

have over the centuries, haven't they? Prophets and saints and such-like."

"Fair enough," said Mr. Sizer breezily. He was, I decided the breeziest person I had ever met. "A rum set-up all the same."

I fetched Caesar a bucket of water and, when the vet had gone, I called the Hermit. Standing on his doorstep, the rain behind me, I told him what the vet had done and recommended. After a moment he said:

"There are some old sheep hurdles back of the barn and a coil of wire hanging up, and plenty of baling string —you can make a barricade with those—wire cutters? Hang on a minute I've a pair in the scullery. There you are."

It was a struggle, but I managed after an hour to fence off the hay and then I rode for home on my iron steed, feeling much more cheerful. The rain was on my back now and the wind blew me along, and overhead the sky lightened, the clouds rising with my spirits, until a ragged patch of blue lay to the west.

After lunch I persuaded Mum that it wasn't worth me returning to school, and then I spent a pleasant afternoon birdwatching in a copse, and so the day ended happily after all, although I could not rid myself of the feeling that some Divine Being had chosen to punish me for selfishness and arrogance by causing Caesar to fall in that stony lane.

CHAPTER FOUR

THE wound healed quickly and well leaving only a small scar.

The Easter holidays came in with wild winds and brittle sunshine and we spent all our spare time down at the Hermit's field, riding, grooming and talking to Caesar. We felt he was our very own. He was also our latest craze, replacing all earlier passions and interests. He was, with his soft eyes, gentle manners and noble expression, a very likeable horse. In a childish way we adored him.

Some of the boys in my class were already going with girls, but I had not found any to match our Mum and Sophie, whom, with their fair hair and periwinkle eyes, looked slightly Scandinavian. Girls of my own age irritated me and I felt no inclination to take their hands or stare into their eyes across formica-topped café tables. Sophie, however, was keen on Chris Langton, although she pretended to our parents that her interest was entirely in Mustard and Cress, for fear, I suppose, that she might otherwise be teased. Chris was almost fourteen, tall for his age with beechnut-brown eyes, thick dark hair and somewhat bulbous lips framing a set of near-perfect teeth, which had not yet experienced the horrors of a dentist's drill. He was a fine cricketer for his age and had gained his silver medal swimming survival test and was working for his gold. Sophie contrived to see him most evenings, picked his brains on the subject of riding and I am afraid told him some of the secrets she had extracted from the Hermit about his past.

By April we were becoming accustomed to our frail friend's strange habits. We took him more or less for granted and treated him like someone of our own age, never mincing our words or adapting our stories as we did sometimes with other grown-ups, even our parents. We hardly noticed his change of habit when he came through the gate, stood in the field and showed us how to pick out Caesar's feet and when one day he patted me on the head, by way of congratulation after Caesar had completed a serpentine, I hardly flinched.

Another day we were riding in the field under a steely grey sky rumbling with thunder, the air heavy with the threat of rain, and the birds without song. As Sophie took Caesar up to the far end under the shelter of the copse, the lightning came, a jagged poker of fire, and clouds darkened the sky as though dusk had come. The rain started, like tears at first, but swiftly turned into a flood that soaked us to the skin. Our hair hung in unsightly rats' tails and the water dripped from the sleeves of our coats. We were not afraid. We were country children used to storms, high winds and dark nights. But we scurried to the barn to seek shelter leading Caesar who bowed his head against the wind, walking crabwise. The Hermit came out, wearing an old sou-wester of black oilskin, his nose protruding underneath like an eagle's beak. He put his thin white hands, which had not known work for many a day, on Caesar's glistening neck and said,

"Rub him down and then come in and warm yourselves by the fire. You must dry out before you go home or what will your poor mother say?"

"Thanks," said Sophie, "I like your hat, it's fantastic. You look like a trawler man."

"Not tough enough," said the Hermit shortly, a drip of rain shining on the very tip of his nose and destroying his dignity.

46

We rubbed Caesar with hay and with the stable rubber until our arms ached, and then I said,

"We promised we wouldn't."

"We couldn't be so mean. Remember how we felt after we had refused those biscuits? We tried to convince ourselves that we had been right by imagining all sorts of awful terrors, thinking up terrible things about the poor man."

"The police said . . ." I began.

"Mum only said it would be *wiser* not to go inside the house. We've got to weigh up the dangers. We are soaked —pneumonia or the faintest chance that the Hermit might. . . ." her voice trailed away; she couldn't now imagine our friend trying to hurt us in any way at all.

"I admit," I said, "that it does seem unfair that someone can't become a simple recluse without everyone suspecting he's bonkers or evil or something."

"He's blameless. I'm sure he's blameless. And there's two of us and remember the judo Dad taught us last year. My teeth are chattering, so are yours. You look ever so funny. Come on."

So we went indoors. The place smelt damp and the shabby rather dark walls were hung with old sporting prints, some foxed. A bright coal fire, fortified with wood, was burning in a Victorian grate. It was for us a novel sight.

"Draw near," said the Hermit. "Warm yourselves." He nodded towards the fire. "Great company on grey days. I'm like a cat staring into the flames, weaving spells and seeing visions, reading my fortune."

I wondered whether he meant days when the weather was grey or when his thoughts were grey.

"Come on, off with your socks and shoes, put them to dry or you'll catch your death of cold. I'll make us all hot Bovril, yes, that's what I'll do. Used to enjoy it when

47

I was a boy after a long bike ride on the Downs. Nothing like a good mug of Bovril, except a nip of brandy and you're a bit young for that. I only keep a bit in the cupboard for medicinal purposes."

"What does he mean?" asked Sophie, when the Hermit had padded off into the back regions of the house.

"Medicinal, medicine, when he's ill."

"Don't let's take off more than our shoes, socks and sweaters," said Sophie nervously.

We examined the contents of the room; the carpets were very worn. Looking back now with more knowledge, I suppose they were Turkish carpets, which had once been very expensive. I was at the age of putting a value on everything and at the time they seemed worthless, and, in my inexperienced eyes, the pictures were only fit for a jumble sale, and the chairs, which needed upholstering, just right for the junk shops. There was a lot of tarnished silver around which I mistook for tin, and two faded photographs of horses, one grey which must have been Skylark, and a black with a beautiful head adorned with a white mark, not a star, but diamond shaped, on the forehead. We thought these photographs the most interesting objects in the room, which smelt deliciously of burning wood—apple wood, we decided.

We scurried back to the fire when we heard the Hermit padding back in his leather slippers. He carried two earthenware pots of steaming Bovril, which he put in the grate before returning to fetch one for himself.

"How do we drink it?" asked my sister. "He said *mugs* but these are not *mugs*; they are soup bowls, and where are the spoons?"

"By the handles at the side, ninny," I said.

"Don't call me that or I shall bash you," said Sophie, but she was laughing and dancing up and down from one leg to another to send the blood racing to warm herself.

With her fair wet hair all about her face, she looked quite primitive.

The Hermit returned, sat down in a shabby leather arm-chair.

"Drink up!" he said, "but go carefully. It's frightfully hot. We don't want scalded mouths do we? That would be an awful catastrophe."

He stared at us so hard that we became embarrassed.

"Sorry," he said. "I didn't meant to gaze at you. It's not often I see children close up, and I was thinking that you were bigger but not sturdier than we were at your age. It's all the protein you eat. Porridge and bread were our staple diet, and plenty of mashed potatoes, milk puddings, sago and tapioca and other nursery horrors. It's all changed since then—awfully interesting—I mean from a scientific and I suppose sociological point of view."

"Do you have a newspaper?" asked Sophie, who wasn't the least interested in science of sociology at that time. "I mean, perhaps you ought to keep more up to date with things going on. Well, do you?" She went close to him, peered into his bony, uncherished face.

"Who would bring me a paper now? They don't deliver right down here, and Mr. Perks only comes Fridays."

"We will!" Sophie and I cried in unison. "Well, why not? Easy. We come every day to feed Caesar. Our paper boy delivers our parents' paper before half past seven so we can order one for you to come at the same time. It's a cinch."

"It's awfully kind of you," began the Hermit diffidently.

"Don't you want to know what's happening? Don't you care?" asked Sophie, warming to her subject, beginning to see this as the beginning of a campaign to bring our friend back into touch with the world.

"I had a wireless once, but it broke," admitted the Hermit, rather sheepishly, withdrawing further into the chair, so that we could only see the tip of his nose.

"I'll mend it or Dad will. Dad's brilliant with radios. He has nimble fingers. He's fabulous," I said.

"He knows you come here then?"

"Yes, why not?" I asked. "What's there to worry about? He's grateful to you for letting us ride Caesar. It gets us from under our Mum's feet, for one thing, and for another, it, well, um, well it makes us very happy."

"I often think," said the Hermit slowly, leaning forward again, so that we could see the whole of his skeleton-like profile, "I often think that if my son was alive and your age I wouldn't let him visit an old man living alone, unless I knew a great deal about that man, and I've wondered whether or not you have been coming here secretly. It's been nagging my mind just a little bit. When you live alone you have a lot of time for thinking."

"Dad checked with the police," Sophie said, and I could have kicked her. The statement seemed an insult, cold, bald, even cruel.

"That was a wise move, I suppose. And of course there is no evidence against me of any sort. I won't say I've led a blameless life. We all have things in our past we regret. But nothing criminal, nothing frightful, just tiny omissions, little sins, no more. There's no murky past, rest assured. Nothing wrong except that I can't go out. I should fall down if I did. Fearful palpitations, heart and all that. But having you around has made me see how lonely I've been. It's made me look back and relive my own childhood. And it's made me think about my son, Nigel, that's something I haven't done for years. I sort of pushed him into a cupboard in my mind and locked the door, turned the key. Well, now I've let him out again, if you see what I mean. It's made me come to terms with, well, with fate if you

50

like, with grief, too. It's helped." He slipped back into the chair again.

"That's great! I'm so glad," cried Sophie, rushing into words to hide her embarrassment.

"Well, I wouldn't use the word *'great'* myself, Sophie, although I notice the word is a favourite with you children. I would say 'that's encouraging', or something like that. It would be more accurate, wouldn't it, more precise?"

"I think you're fabulous," said Sophie, "and I'm sorry if I can't find the right way of saying things. Perhaps I will soon, next year when I'm twelve perhaps."

"But I'm not a child," I said, "I'm really a teenager, although it doesn't feel like that, and I'm not crazy on gear or pop and all that. My birthday is not far away— June 25th, actually."

"I'm June 24th," said the Hermit. "What a coincidence. Both Cancer, but I wish I wasn't really, do you, Matthew? Because of the name. It's a lovely star but we've named that dreadful disease after it. I wonder why? It's an awful shame really. You know we ought to have a joint birthday celebration, just before midnight on the 24th. I would open my presents just before the stroke of midnight and you just after. Wouldn't it be fun?" He paused a moment smiling, his eyes suddenly alive. The deathly look in his thin face had gone. It was as though ten years had been wiped off his life and he was in his forties, and while he spoke he waved his thin white hands in the air; like a bird clawing wildly to get his grip again on some perch. They were the colour of alabaster. I must have looked nervous. I was wondering what my parents would say at such a suggestion. Me in the Hermit's house at midnight, with school next day? But our friend saw this and changed his tone suddenly:

"It's all right, Matthew. I was only joking. Don't take me seriously. I was being a child again, letting my imagin-

51

ation run away with me. Even the most sedate grown-ups do that sometimes, although I admit most of them don't speak such ridiculous flights of fancy aloud. How are those socks and shoes drying? Time for you to go home to lunch, before your mother worries."

We saw suddenly that he was very tired, that the talking had wearied him, and we feared for the tiresome heart which was such a bind. We put on our socks and shoes which were still wet but warm from the fire and carried our sodden sweaters. Our Mum would be angry with us anyway, because we had come without anoraks.

Outside, the storm had passed; the sky had cleared patchily leaving a sea of blue broken by grey rocks and hills tinged with the sun's gold. All the trees glistened with the silver of the rain, and the earth smelled fresh. We turned Caesar loose in the field, and he cantered off tossing his head like a youngster, then stopped pawed the ground knelt down and rolled. When he climbed to his feet again we saw he was filthy with mud, one thin patch jauntily placed half over one eye, giving him a roguish air.

"Monster!" we cried, "Beast!" for we realised we should have to make good use of the dandy brush to make him respectable again.

After that day we came to know the Hermit's house quite well. He gave us many cups of coffee and tea served with powdered milk, and a fizzy lemonade brought in bottles by Mr. Perks. He produced the brands of biscuits which had meant a lot to him in his childhood, which he must have ordered specially from Mr. Perks, and he seemed to derive pleasure from the fact that we were sharing these with him. They were quite ordinary biscuits: gingerbreads, chocolate wheatmeal, digestive, petit beurre and such like. He became more talkative, and it seemed to us that his face was filling out, that he was less—what is the word I want?—corpse-like, cadaverous, sort of ghostly, well, he was less of a zombie. The better we knew the Hermit the more we talked about him. We gained kudos, we thought, by knowing him—after all, nobody else knew him. We even boasted about his intelligence, all the poetry he knew; his pictures, which we had learned were not valueless after all, and his furniture. We wanted him to seem rich and important because then we could bask in reflected glory, and I took to asking him about the value of everything. Often he dismissed it, saying sharply, "Sentimental value cannot be priced." But sometimes when I persisted he would throw out a sum carelessly, "About a hundred," he would say. "Or could be a thousand."

There was a picture in the hall of a black labrador gazing up at a man with a gun, set against a background of hills, which the Hermit said could be worth thousands.

"But I'm hopelessly out of date," he added. "Haven't been in a saleroom for years."

Every morning we took him the *Telegraph*, a fact we let be known in the village, for we wanted everyone to know that this weird man in the ivy-clad house trusted us, that we had broken through his reserve, and succeeded where the local social workers, clergy and do-gooders had failed. After a while the villagers started to treat us as Hermit experts and to ask us questions about our friend which we in our conceit were delighted to answer. What clothes did he wear? Was his house clean? Did he shave? Could he read and write? And such like. And proudly we announced that once he had been married with one son, and that he was an equitation expert, that he owned a number of sporting pictures, dirty but valuable, and much more besides. We let our tongues run away with us and we exaggerated shamelessly, until one day our Mum found us holding forth in the butcher's shop, where we had been sent to buy chops, and she took us aside afterwards and said we should be ashamed of ourselves. Why had we not *respected* the Hermit's privacy? If he had wanted the facts of his past and details of the inside of his house known he would have come out into the village and done it himself. He had trusted us and we were letting him down, simply because we wanted to show off. Anyway, how did we know so much about his house? Had we been peering through the windows like nosey parkers? She was very angry; her eyes, usually so cool, blazed like little fires in her golden sun-tanned face, and, although afterwards we told ourselves that she was furious only because James had kept her up at night, we knew inside that what she said was true and we were filled with remorse. We tried to make it up to the Hermit by all sorts of little kindnesses. We took him bars of Cadbury's milk chocolate, on which he had once told us he had doted as a child. We even found some bullseyes—a round sweet striped black and white tasting slightly of peppermint—which had been popular before the war, and took him a quarter of those. But not knowing of our treachery he was mystified and then embarrassed by these presents and forbade us to spend any of our money on him again. We did enough for him, he said, by bringing him a newspaper and exercising his horse.

Between ourselves we played a game of using the Hermit's words and phrases not in mockery but because it was all part of the time we spent with him and Caesar and in a way, I suppose, precious to us.

"I'm frightfully hot today," I would say, as we cycled home.

"Awfully dusty, isn't it?" Sophie would reply.

"Super day though. By jove! look at those clouds, haven't seen any like that since before the war."

"Not so many cars about then, quieter. I say, thanks

terribly for the lunch. It was tremendous, awfully kind of you."

We had noticed that the war was the great dividing line. Before the war and after the war were two different worlds for the Hermit; one in which he could live; the other in which he could not. It was very strange.

Meanwhile our schooling of Caesar had become more serious and now included jumping. At first he had refused everything with a determination which we could not understand, putting down his head, digging in his toes and nearly throwing us off. Then we took to tempting him over with sugar. It wasn't a method recommended in any book we had read, but it seemed to work and after a bit we discovered he could jump extremely well if he felt inclined. He was very greedy and would stop immediately he cleared a fence and whinny softly for his sugar and he wouldn't move another step until he had eaten it. For a time he expected sugar after every fence, so there wasn't much hope of completing a course without stopping.

Gradually the Hermit took to coming right out into the field to give us hints. He was, we thought, a little old-fashioned and we discovered that he had been taught to jump as a boy with the *Weedon seat*, a jumping position used by the British Army at that time when riders were trained at a big depot at a place called Weedon. With this seat you bobbed down to one side as the horse took off and came down in the saddle as he landed. We, nevertheless, followed the *Pony Club Manual*, putting our weight in our knees and thighs, pressing down into our heels and placing our hands either side of Caesar's neck so that there was a straight line from our elbows to Caesar's mouth. When the jumps were over two feet we shortened our stirrups two holes, so that we could approach the jump with our buttocks off the saddle. After a while the Hermit stopped suggesting the Weedon methods and accepted our forward seat as modern. He also knew about point-to-pointing, for which, he said, he had ridden more wildly without attempting the Weedon seat, but adapting himself to the horse's movements. "Sometimes I only stayed on by the grace of God," he admitted with a wry smile.

Very soon we realised that Caesar was a trained jumper long before he fell into our hands, and that he could easily clear jumps of four feet or more if he wanted a lump of sugar, and we began to wonder more and more about his past. How had he come into the hands of the Hermit's sister, who only bought old crocks, broken and ill-treated animals which needed nursing back into health and sanity?

The Hermit said he would write to ask, even though such an action would fill his sister with a sense of triumph, which he would resent because he wanted to live his own life as he chose and not as his sister decreed.

"Tell me," he said, "is there anything wrong with a man deciding that he wants to retire into his own house and live a quiet life alone apart from his fellow beings? Does it smack of something disagreeable? Must that man be prevented from such a course of action? If so, why? This is supposed to be a free country, isn't it? We fought the war to preserve that freedom, didn't we? No doubt if Hitler had won I might have been destroyed as a useless specimen unable to fulfil his work quota—the gas oven or the firing squad might have been mine. But he didn't win, so why shouldn't I live as I want. I'm not doing anyone any harm. I'm just a sort of hedgehog."

"Yes, of course," we said. "You are right to live as you like. Yes, we agree, absolutely."

"But, of course," he went on, "she will think she's won the first round. She'll be cock-a-whoop, sure that her little plan has worked. And I don't want her down here bossing me around. You know what elder sisters can be? Still, I *will* write, just to please you."

"Thank you," we chorused.

I wondered vaguely how I would feel towards Sophie in years to come, for, in her way, she wanted to boss me, too, even to mother me sometimes, and I had to fight against it or I found myself tagging after her like some little kid. One of the things I liked especially about the Hermit was the way he saw this and put a stop to it. He always said "Ladies first," when it came to doorways and such like, but when it came to really important and exciting actions he said, "Eldest first." And that pleased me. Perhaps he saw in me a version of his own boyhood or, perhaps he saw Nigel and all that might have been except for . . . except for what? It was an answer we did not have, and the village gossips were irked by our lack of success in this quarter. They speculated: "Divorced," they suggested, for it would be difficult for a woman to live happily with such a strange man. Mother and son both killed in a road accident. Such terrible things happened on the roads these days. And a man like the Hermit, so cut-off, weird, couldn't have been much of a driver—too timid, no doubt. The timid caused as many accidents as the reckless. And so on and on. But, ashamed of our previous treachery, we gave nothing away. Our tongues were tied, we said importantly, as though we knew all, and then we closed up like sea anenomes when you try to touch their red petals.

Now Caesar's hoofs were beginning to split, and the Hermit said it was time the horse was shod and would we see to it? Sophie persuaded Chris, to write down the name of the local blacksmith, who told us to bring Caesar down to the Langton's farm in three days' time when he would be shoeing Mustard and Cress. The Hermit said:

"What an admirable arrangement. But how much is it?"

"One pound ten, old currency, one fifty new," said Sophie.

"And it used to be six shillings when I was a boy, plus a sixpenny tip. Scandalous! Don't you think it's scandalous?"

"I suppose the cost of iron has gone up," I suggested. "Or steel or whatever it is."

Sophie said, "Bags ride Caesar to be shod."

But the Hermit said I was to take the horse, because as it was only the second time we had tried him on the road, he might be frightened of traffic, and I was larger and older than Sophie.

"Never worry, young lady, your turn will come. You can ride him back if he behaves well going over."

Sophie made a face, but said nothing. To tell the truth she hated to be called "young lady". Don't ask me why. It seemed a harmless enough form of address, but it irked her. "I'm not a lady," she would say, "I'm a girl, and one day I suppose I will have to be a woman, although I'm in no hurry to grow up. I would like to be a teenager for years and years."

Actually, Caesar behaved excellently on the road and took no notice of traffic, even ignoring a wild gang of leather-clad motor cyclists who came roaring by. And he stood like an angel while he was shod.

"A good sort," said the blacksmith. "Where did you find him? Must be worth a pretty penny?"

"He's not ours," I said, "he belongs to an elderly gentleman."

"To the weird old man down the lane, old looney, goofy," said Jane, to my fury.

"Ah, the chap they call the Hermit. Strange fellow. But I've not heard it said that he's mental like, just withdrawn, and we all feel like doing that sometimes, what with the noise and the smell and all the busybodies. So this is his horse, is it? A smashing horse by the look of him. I don't want to be curious, don't answer if you'd rather not, but does the old man ride it?"

"No, we do," said Sophie. "He's just given him a good home, he's a throw-out or something."

"A horse with a past," I said.

"Go on!" said the blacksmith, turning his grimy, heat-tanned face back to his portable anvil.

In spite of Jane's nastiness that day we let her try Caesar in the farm meadow by the house, after Chris had enjoyed his turn, and both the Langtons were impressed by his long stride and beautiful head carriage. They said he was fabulous and what was his past? We repeated that we did not know and then, remembering Mum's fury, we shut up and changed the subject to swimming, which was a Langton craze.

Sophie rode Caesar back while I pedalled along on her cycle. She was so happy that she sang blithely and, as if in keeping with our mood, the sun came out and, through the young leaves, dappled the lane with gold. The birds were busy darting here and there with straw for nests or food for young, trilling in the trees and building in the hedges. All around were the sweet scents of spring and the warm softness of April. It was a day when hopes are high, when for a moment time seems to stand still and you feel you could catch your happiness and hold it in your hand, and say to the world "this is it. This is perfect."

But of course the moment doesn't last. This time the aura of happiness fell apart with our return to the ivy-clad house, when we saw the Hermit waiting at the gate for us. And it seemed to me then that the sun, so kind to the beautiful, is often cruel to the old, the shabby and the ill. For, standing there in the golden sunlight, the Hermit looked like a skeleton dressed up in clothes for some strange rite, a broken man encased in a skin grown too large for his bones like a cheap sweater stretched too far on a washing line; eyes like stones, a tortoise mouth grim and primeval. We stared, our stomachs tightening into knots. He beckoned rather wildly like a madman alone in some deserted place calling to strange figures of his imagination, his mouth moving soundlessly in agitation. Suddenly we feared that he was much iller than we had supposed when we had ignored his suffering and fussy references to palpitations.

"Come," he said, waving a telegram in his hand. "Come quickly there's news."

We went to the gate and Sophie dismounted.

"What is it, Mr. Hermit? What is the matter? Something dreadful?" It was the first time we had called him Mr. Hermit, but he didn't seem to care.

"Nothing," he said, drooping a little like a stale stalk of cow parsley caught by the wind. "Just my sister up to her tricks. Look at this."

He handed me the telegram. I read: *So glad the horse is a success. Please go to Frinkley Station and meet the four o'clock train from Chatham to collect a live parcel—Hester.*

"How could she expect *me* to go? What madness is the silly woman up to now? And what is the live parcel—a cow, horse, giraffe? Or some freak like a diseased or deformed lion? One horse is enough and I couldn't manage him without the help of you, my ministering angels."

Talking helped him. He was calmer; he moved back into the shade and the kinder light seemed to bring life back into his cheeks.

"Not angels," I said quickly, remembering our repeated treachery.

"We'll get the live parcel. What fun! How fantastic!" cried Sophie, jumping up and down. "What's the time?"

"Three thirty five. We can make Frinkley station in half

an hour on our cycles if we ride like the wind, easily. Here, you must unsaddle Caesar." I took the reins from Sophie and handed them to the Hermit. "See you!"

The next moment we were on our cycles racing down the lane. We took the hump-backed bridge so fast that our tummies were left behind.

"Could it be a newt—a crested newt—or an otter, a rare lizard or baby crocodile, something really exciting?" I wondered.

"More likely a stray cat with poor mangy fur and diseased runny eyes," said Sophie gloomily. "Still it would be wonderful to nurse it back to health to see it growing plumper and prouder day by day, until it boasted a glistening coat and large placid eyes and a purr as loud as an engine. I say, slow up, will you? My legs are shorter than yours. I'm puffed out."

"I wish we had a really good biology master at school, a sort of Gerald Durrell, someone who could tell us how to look after a baby crocodile or a snake or whatever it is going to be—a parrot perhaps who has outlived the old lady who owned it."

"It's bound to be a cat. There are dozens of cats needing homes. Really it's the Hermit's duty to have one. Well, isn't it? I mean with all that land and a barn. *And* I've heard mice around."

"Awfully nice of you to mention it, but frankly I'd rather not," I said imitating the Hermit's voice.

Frinkley was a small Kentish market town, modest once with a square surrounded by houses built for moderately successful merchants, but now mainly redeveloped with plenty of glass and concrete, two tall office blocks and a new supermarket, library and post office. Beyond them on a hill a shabby row of Victorian houses had survived to look down across the river in the valley like frowning grandparents. I thought them more interesting than the modern blocks, because some of them had little turrets and coach houses with arches and decorative stone work over the doors and windows.

Below them, behind the supermarket, an Edwardian station was tucked away like some tramp hiding from a group of young people in the trendiest gear. Red brick, almost deserted, it looked shabby and neglected. But to the left of it was a crowded car park which proved that it was still well used during rush hours to bear the Frinkley folk away to offices, shops and factories nearer to London.

The train from Chatham had come and gone. The platform was empty, a gentle wind whistled down the line. But in the Parcels Office we found a crate with a barred front in which sat a black and tan mongrel with apologetic eyes and a tail that moved slowly and timidly, as though the little dog did not know whether she should welcome us as friends. On the crate was a label addressed to Mr. Patrick Piers and another saying *To Be Collected*, and a third saying *Livestock with Care*, as if everyone could not see the dog inside.

"You're a live parcel," I said.

"She's *sweet*," said Sophie. "Look at those fabulous eyes. Perhaps we could have her if she's too much for the Hermit."

"You know we can't. You know she will give James an attack. So come off it! Come down to earth! How are we going to get her back to the Hermit. We can't carry that crate. It's enormous."

"Lead her, of course. Buy her a leash."

"We haven't brought any money, nincompoops that we are!"

"A bit of string then."

There were footsteps, a little cough.

"Hi, you two, OUT. Do you hear me, out, scram, beat it!" A railway man stared us in the face, weatherbeaten, cross and stout, a pencil behind his ear and a cap on the back of his head.

"Cheek!" said Sophie.

"But . . ." I began.

"And no messing. We've had enough of young vandals here already. Do you want me to call the police?"

I glanced at Sophie and then at myself. We were incredibly dirty; our corduroy trousers grey with dust and inside the legs dark with Caesar's dried sweat; our faces smudged with black from poking amongst the blacksmith's tools. Then I stood up very straight, pushed back my spectacles and, trying to sound very dignified, said,

"Mr. Patrick Piers sent us to fetch his dog as a matter of fact."

"Oh, he has, has he, sent a letter with you, has he? We must have proof of identification; we don't hand over valuable goods to every Tom, Dick or Harry who comes along."

"No letters," I admitted sadly. "He only got his sister's wire at two and he didn't do anything until we came back from the blacksmiths. He's not very well, you see, doesn't go out any more; that's why he asked us to come. He was a bit desperate, actually."

"You his children, then?"

"No, just friends."

"A likely story."

"Oh, please, just because we look scruffy don't misjudge us. It's not right to judge by appearances is it? Fine feathers don't always make fine birds—that's what our only Grannie says and it's true, isn't it?" Sophie looked up at the railway man with a smile; her eyes sparkled and through the dirt her cheeks seemed to glow. "Of course you've got to be careful, especially with such a dear little dog . . . but . . ."

The man gave a half smile, then straightened his face

again, remembering his duty to protect the railway's customers from young hooligans of both sexes.

"Where's the dog come from? Who sent it? What train were you supposed to meet? Let's have chapter and verse."

"Train from Chatham due to arrive here four p.m., sent by," I dithered. Was the Hermit's sister married? I thought probably not. "Miss Piers as a present for her invalid brother who lives alone, she has already sent a horse, by the way."

"Never mind about the horse. Address of sender?"

"An animal home," I said quickly. "I forget the name. Somewhere for lost, deserted and ill animals, a sanctuary."

"Address of new owner."

We gave the Hermit's address and saw that at last the railway man was satisfied. He pulled the pencil from behind his ear just like Mr. Perks in the *Railway Children*, and asked us to sign a rather grubby form. Then Sophie asked if he could spare a piece of cord, string or rope, as we were going to lead the dog to her new home.

"It's a long walk," said the railway man. "I'll see what I can do."

He went away and came back with about three feet of white cord. "Is that long enough?"

"Great, thank you."

"About the crate," he said. "Will you be needing it?"

We said we didn't think so, and then the railway man told us he kept racing pigeons, and he could convert it into another hutch. "Good strong crate, that."

We parted a few moments later on very friendly terms and within ten minutes Sophie and I were on the outskirts of the town heading for the Hermit's house.

The dog had a feathery tail which she carried erect when she was excited, and soft feathered ears tipped and lined a rich tan, and eyes so appealing that we thought

64

they would soften the hardest heart. She was mainly black but with the most beautiful tan shadings. tan knees, tan hocks, tan plus fours and loveliest of all tan arches above her eyes and a tan muzzle. Her nose was fine, delicate and pointed and, although she was only a mongrel, the word exquisite would not be out of place in describing her. After much musing and a couple of minor arguments we decided she was probably part whippet, part collie and part lakeland terrier.

It was now five and a half miles to the Hermit's house and the light of day was being sucked from the little streets through which we were passing. We had no lamps on our cycles which we pushed. It was dark when we reached the hump-backed bridge. Dusk had come and gone and night lay like black felt across the landscape.

"I wish there was a moon," said Sophie. "I'm not keen on the darkness." She sighed. "It's awfully spooky."

But our eyes soon became accustomed to the night and we could see well enough to keep on the road. Little nocturnal noises broke the silence: the moving of cattle in the grass; the soft crunch of bovine teeth; the wind whispering in the elms and the scurry of small animals—shrew mice, field mice, voles, stoats? Or simply birds shifting on their perches of stick, twig or thorn? We could not tell. Sophie shivered. "I wish there wasn't a ditch; things can hide in ditches."

"Nonsense."

Now and then she gasped or gave a little shriek, more I think from surprise than actual fear. Presently, farther down the valley where the trees stood thick and still, blacker than the night, owls started to hoot, then flew across the sky crying as they went. We seemed to hear the whir of their wings. The little dog barked, three sharp yaps, a terrier's bark, and she strained at the cord.

At last we saw the outline of the Hermit's house, solid

C

and silent, although in its ivy there was a live and moving world of insects, and we heard now the sharp squeak of bats as they went about their business guided by their internal radar system.

"When I'm older I shall come here with a camera and flash bulbs and photograph those bats," I announced. "How many O levels do I need to be a photographer?"

"I haven't the foggiest notion."

"That's the Hermit's phrase."

"Yes, I know, well why not? You borrow his words sometimes."

In the field we could just make out Caesar's chunky outline as he stood drowsing by one of those stark, stripped trees that shone white like sun bleached tombs in the desert. Hearing our voices, Caesar let out a long welcoming neigh and all at once the silent, brooding house seemed to come ablaze with light. The Hermit stood on his doorstep, bright-eyed and anxious, his hands gesticulating. I thought then that if he was a real hermit he wouldn't have electricity but candles; for electric power in the house meant meter readers and inspectors, and real hermits wanted no contacts with humans at all.

We threw down our cycles.

"So it's a dog," the Hermit said. "The old devil, the monkey, and I nearly had a heart attack thinking it was something much more difficult, a prickly porcupine, a dangerous leopard or something. So she's been and gone and sent me a dog. A bitch, I suppose?"

We said "yes," and then he said he would bet his last dollar that she was in whelp. "That's when the cads throw the poor little devils out, just when they need most support and comfort. She's lucky she wasn't drowned."

"She doesn't look at all fat," Sophie said.

"It's true," said the Hermit. "We must just wait and see. How goes the enemy?"

"My watch has stopped. It must be past seven," I said.

"You children can never keep your watches wound. I don't know how you would ever get along on a desert island, I really don't."

"But we've no wish to be stranded on desert-islands," said Sophie.

"I have if it's one with humming birds, parrots, monkeys, bananas and all that," I said.

The Hermit crouched down on his knees, clicked his second finger and thumb together, whistled and said,

"Come along, my little beauty. Come, my little darling." And now with the light behind him, his worries gone, he looked much younger than earlier in the day, and there was even something boyish in the way he smiled as the little dog approached him, her tail low, wagging ever so gently; her eyes watching his face; her body poised both for a rebuff and a welcome. At that moment Sophie and I were like fond parents watching their favourite child react to a new pet; and we saw that the Hermit's sister was a wiser woman than we had supposed, that in her way she was helping to mend her brother's damaged life in the best way she could. Then my thoughts were interrupted by the purr and rumble of a car and the blackness behind us was broken by the glow of headlights. There was a little scuffling sound in the hedgerow and then the Hermit picked up the dog, hurried into the house and shut the rotten door.

The car came to a stop and out jumped our Dad.

"Children!" he shouted, his voice breaking brutally into the softness of the night. "You've thrown your cycles down on the edge of the road. Do you *want* them run over? Do you know how much cycles cost? Are you daft?"

"Twenty to thirty pounds a cycle now, I suppose," I said. "Sorry Dad. We didn't think."

"Your mother has been mad with worry. Do you know what the time is?"

"After seven."

In contrast with the Hermit, Dad looked overweight, strong enough to knock down a wall with his bare hands. His big wide face was red with anger.

"Don't stand there staring. Pick the cycles up. Come on, get moving. You've no lights and no torch. This is the last time you come down here. Do you understand?" The punishment did not seem to fit the crime. It was unfair, too harsh. Sophie began to cry, whimpering, as she stood her cycle up. Caesar came to the gate and whinnied softly; we could see his breath warm in the cool April night. Standing near him we could feel the heat of his body. His winter coat had almost gone and his summer one shone like polished mahogany; etched against the ink dark night, his head had noble rough-hewn beauty as though carved from stone. He was great; he was the greatest thing in our lives.

"Is this the beast?" asked Dad, his voice softer.

"That's Caesar," I said. "He's fantastic and awfully kind." Sophie blew her nose.

"Awfully and kind don't go together," Dad said sternly. "How do you get on the brute, by step ladder?"

"Off the gate."

"He's not really a brute, Dad," objected Sophie. "Really he isn't. He's ever so good. You've no idea . . ." She sniffed again.

"'Cor bless me, look at those feet," said Dad. "Shouldn't want one of them on my toes."

"He's too gentle to step on feet," I said.

"The gentle giant, is that it?"

Dad was thawing. We couldn't feel his anger any longer.

Sophie leaned against the gate and Caesar started to search her pockets for sugar. He possessed an extra long,

lightly whiskered upper lip, exceptionally mobile, yet delicate, like a giraffe's.

"You're tickling," said Sophie giggling through her
tears.

"He seems to like you," said Dad. "Where's the old
man?"

"Gone inside. You frightened him."

I wasn't annoyed with the Hermit for leaving us to ex-
plain. It seemed quite natural; he could not cope with life,
so we had to cope for him.

I started to tell Dad about the telegram and the dog.
Now and then Sophie interrupted me when she thought I
was glossing over something or leaving something out.
When I had finished Dad looked quite amused. He even
allowed himself half a smile.

"Quite an eccentric," he said. "Next time in emergen-
cies of that kind enlist your parents' help. Right?"

"Right."

"I'm going to be home a good deal for the next week
or so. We've been called out on strike. It's a load of rubbish, but I'm not going into the ins and outs now. There
it is. No work tomorrow, nor the next day, nor the day
after, that I can see. So mind how you go, cos' I shall be
around to pull you up. Now put your cycles away somewhere and I'll run you home."

"We must just give Caesar his hay," said Sophie.

We fetched two large armfuls for him from the barn
and put them by the elderberry tree under which he could
take shelter if it rained. Usually we filled him a net, but
we didn't like to keep Dad waiting, especially with Mum
worrying at home, and now that spring had come the new
grass was through and Caesar only needed a little hay
night and morning.

We didn't say anything more about the horse on the way
home, although we suspected that Dad had relented and

if we kept quiet and were especially good and helpful we would still be allowed to ride. And we gave the full credit for the reversed decision to Caesar, his whinny of welcome, his searching upper lip and his handsomeness. We asked tactful questions about the strike and when we saw Mum Sophie threw herself gratefully into her arms, and I apologised and, to our surprise Dad started to make excuses for us. He also said that he would buy us lights for our cycles the next morning, but we must pay him back out of our pocket money.

CHAPTER FIVE

As spring turned into summer and the sun climbed higher in the sky, the Hermit seemed to grow stronger. He came outside more often and his paper-white face took on new shades of pink, cream and sand. He became more of a man, solid.

Sometimes he stood in the middle of the field and taught us, his rusty voice rising occasionally to a shout of exasperation or praise. The little dog, adoring and faithful, delighted with her new home, would stand beside him; her soft eyes watching us. He called her Katie after a dog he had known in his youth. She was not in whelp.

The Hermit's sister wrote in reply to his letter, saying that she had bought Caesar for fifty pounds, carcase price, without a warranty. He had a poor reputation. A neurotic rebel, he had been pitifully thin, riddled with worms, the largest mount at a Welsh pony trekking centre which had been closed down as a result of action taken by the R.S.P.C.A. Caesar, she wrote, had started life as a jumper, but had lost his nerve early through being over-faced and rapped, becoming soured by the equine rat race. Eventually he had refused even to enter a show ring. He had learned to rear and his greedy owners, who had hoped to sell him as a trained jumper for at least a thousand pounds, grew cruel and angry. They used spurs and a cutting whip, but Caesar's mind was made up. He would never jump for them again. They despaired after two years and sold him to a riding school, but, by then he knew his power, and after a year he rebelled, rearing whenever he was asked to enter the covered school. He was tired of men and women who did not know how to ride, who gave him signals he did not understand and hung on to his mouth. But he had never objected to hacking through the countryside, so the riding school owners sold him for eighty pounds to the pony trekking centre, an infamous place, where during the summer holiday season horses and ponies were worked to death carrying tourists, many of whom had never taken a riding lesson in their lives. It was the aim of the pony trekking centre owners to make a thousand pounds in the eight weeks between mid-July and September. Often their animals would be out on the hills from ten until four on an all-day trek and then be used for evening rides as well. At night they could not rest because they had to graze to fill their empty stomachs before morning, for they were given no feeds during the day. When an R.S.P.C.A. Inspector was sent to investigate the Centre he found three ponies were suffering from horse flu, four were still working, although lame, and no less than five were suffering from sores caused by ill fitting saddlery. Caesar was simply very thin and tired with a dry cough. Two of the ponies were so diseased that they had to be put-down, others were found homes. It was Miss Piers's friend at the R.S.P.C.A. office in London who wrote suggesting that she might like to take the big horse with the Roman nose, who was hard to find a good home because of his condition and size. She had arranged for him to be photographed and then had persuaded an old lady to donate fifty pounds for his purchase.

"The poor horse has been hopelessly misunderstood," she wrote. "A little love, a little understanding and patience, and he will be at least a mount for you to ride around the Kent countryside, and bring back to you the happiness of those old far off days before the war."

On receiving this letter the Hermit immediately sent a cheque for fifty pounds to his sister. "Now Caesar is properly ours," he said.

And now almost against our will a dream grew in our hearts larger and larger until it burst open into words like a bud into blossom under the summer sun. It warmed us and drew the three of us closer together. *We would train Caesar for the Frinkley Show.* "We will show everybody what kindness can do," the Hermit said.

We were united. From his house, garden and field, the Hermit organised the campaign, his dicky heart almost, it seemed, forgotten. He wrote letters ordering timber for jumps, gave us money to buy joinery tools, saddle soap, hoof oil and yards and yards of rope. He took to slipping out in the field in the oddest hours to observe Caesar as he grazed or stood dreaming under the elderberry tree where the last creamy rosettes of flower were turning into hard green berries to ripen red in the August sun. He set me to work with Dad's hook to clear the weedy patches in the field and, handing me a brand new saw, ordered me to cut down the two dead trees, stripped so long ago of bark, which we had christened Isaac and Esau. I didn't want them to go; they had become a landmark for Sophie and I and were part of the aura that surrounded the Hermit's place, but the Hermit would brook no argument.

"Nothing but sentiment. They get in the way. You don't

72

get trees in a show ring, do you? Tommyrot—that's what I say—tommyrot."

Dry as cork, brittle as old bones, they came down without a sound, not even a creak. "Been dead years," the Hermit said.

He wanted every inch of the field for Caesar—the elderberry must stay to give him shade—and he wanted the turf smooth as turf in the show ring and the ground level as a football field. He talked of events regular features of horsey life before the war but long ago defunct—Olympia, Richmond and others I cannot now recall. We filled in rabbit holes, dug up old tree stumps with a mattock, cut back brambles and trimmed the thorn hedges, snipping off the last of the white flowers which lay like clotted cream amongst the bright greenness of their leaves. The naturalist in me rebelled a little. How many insects' homes had we destroyed? The old tree stumps had held a whole community of little insects, running this way and that in alarm as the mattock struck. Where would they go now? Who else allowed stumps like these to break the smooth tidiness of well tended land? Blisters came on my hands and at night my arms ached, and once the P.E. teacher at school, a small sarcastic man with toothbrush moustache, asked me why I was so stiff, and another boy said; "It's all the riding he does. He's a great jockey, is Matthew." He made galloping motions and three other boys laughed. But I thought, "you wait, I'll show you. You wait for the Frinkley Show."

There were reports in the village of the Hermit being seen out in striped pyjamas at midnight staring across the field in the light of the silver moon, and also at milking time, half dressed. People wondered whether he was losing his reason altogether. But Sophie and I knew that Caesar had filled a void in an almost empty life and that the show had become an obsession in the Hermit's mind,

73

almost a crusade. And we were glad, because the Hermit's cheeks had grown rounder and pinker, and his eyes had lost that blank look. Most of all, we were pleased because we liked riding and horses and his obsession provided both for us and gave a new purpose to our lives.

The Hermit ordered twenty stakes and I was soon set to making a ring with these and the rope in which to school Caesar. He went round it without jumps kindly enough and we rewarded him with sugar and cubes.

"That horse will be needing a dentist, soon—at the rate he eats sugar," said the Hermit.

Living alone, Caesar had become very attached to us, for we were his only form of company and he took to greeting us as one horse greets another with loud neighs rather than whinnies. Sometimes I was afraid he was sadly cut off from his own kind, but the Hermit said better that than another pony trekking centre or a bullet in the head.

We borrowed instructional books from the library, and in the light of these we decided to school Caesar as much on the flat as over jumps. We taught him the turn on the forehand and then the turns on the haunches or pirouette, and we attempted the shoulder-in, which one author described as "an essential exercise for every jumper widely practised in Europe but sadly neglected by most British riders". The Hermit brushed all this aside, being more interested in getting Caesar fit and trying him over the jumps, which I was making slowly and inexpertly in the evenings.

Dad's firm was still on strike, so he cancelled the Welsh caravan holiday which he had planned for us in September. We were not sorry. We wanted to devote all our spare time to schooling Caesar. After a while, hearing of my poor attempts to make a course of jumps Dad offered to come down one evening to lend a hand, as he put it. He met the Hermit, who became rather wild and nervous, fluttering around with his hands like a bird caught in a room with all the windows shut, so that Sophie and I were a little ashamed of him. But at least he did not run indoors and shut the door, and after a bit, seeing that Dad was more concerned with the principles of carpentry than with him, he calmed down and started nagging Sophie to use the wisp with more energy, to build up Caesar's muscles.

The next person who came to help was Chris Langton, who was missing his evenings with Sophie. More intelligent than I, he was able to help us with some of the more difficult passages in one or two of the books we borrowed, even translating for us the odd German quotation. The Hermit grew to like him enough to ignore him, and then to give him biscuits along with Sophie and I, but never offered Dad a thing. It seemed that grown-ups were out, as far as he was concerned. Katie treated all of us as one of the family, sitting beside us in the grass and offering her delicately shaped paws, which were prettily marked with patches of rich tan.

In early June, as the first blooms broke on the overgrown rose bushes around the house the Hermit suggested that we should start riding Caesar regularly on the road.

"Plenty of jog-trotting up hills to build up his shoulder muscles," he told us, for he had an old-fashioned belief in the value of roadwork to bring a horse into peak condition.

So the village grew accustomed to seeing us on the big bay horse and the questions about the Hermit and his way of life increased; the curiosity of the people sprang again into life like ashes under the bellows, and we found it hard to curb our tongues. Soon the villagers knew about the Hermit's sister, the cheques he wrote and where he banked his money. And Sophie, being both talkative and popular, was worse than me and, no doubt, farther down the valley Chris talked, for what is more exhilarating than possessing information others want and letting it out in dribs and drabs like toothpaste squeezed from its tube? The villagers meant no harm; they were our neighbours and friends and they would have liked to be down there at the ivy-clad house putting the Hermit straight, cleaning the place, tidying the land, and looking at all his things. They imagined many knick knacks; someone had heard a story somewhere that once years and years ago he had been in the Far East, from where, it was rumoured, he had brought back trophies. Some people admired him for taking in an ill-treated horse and a forsaken little dog with silky ears and a soft-eyed look which seemed to point to her need of a protector. Once again we sang his praises.

But, of course, we should not have talked. We had been warned by our parents. But we enjoyed showing off and we were both silly and conceited. We were, as Dad said later, bird brained. As for Mum, poor James had grown worse one night and suffered a fearful attack of asthma. An ambulance came siren blaring and bore him away to hospital so that he could receive oxygen and, after that, there was talk of him going to a special school for asthmatic children in Davos, Switzerland. He was too young now, but his name was put on the waiting list. Meanwhile our Mum watched him anxiously all day like a young and pretty hen with its first chick. The house seemed full of steam kettles, nose sprays, ointments and this and that. We were forced to keep some of the clothes we wore at the Hermit's place away from James, in case the animal hairs and dust brought on a new attack. Otherwise we had to change clothes as soon as we came into the house after riding. Sometimes we were mean enough to be annoyed at having to change. We would shout, "All right," or "In a minute, don't nag," in horrible rude voices and then afterwards we would be remorseful; we would try to make up for our sullen behaviour by helping Mum wash up or by amusing James, who was now a bouncy toddler full of jokes when he wasn't laid low with croup, asthma, eczema or bronchitis. Julie suffered more than us, for she had no refuge and grew disagreeable because she thought Mum loved James more than her, and so she used to throw terrible tantrums to draw attention to herself, lying on the floor and kicking wildly, growing so red in the face that sometimes we thought she must choke. Perhaps she was trying to imitate her little brother in the hope that she might gain the same attention. Her tantrums and James's illnesses did not make for a very calm home life or a mother with a ready ear to listen to stories of our adventures, disasters or disappointments.

The Hermit's place became our escape from all the turmoil and anxieties of home and our Mum hardly noticed when we were late back, unless a meal was spoiling, and rarely had time to ask us about our riding. But at least it was better with Dad away from work, for he shopped and washed up and sent her for an hour's rest every afternoon. He also completed the course of jumps, sometimes bringing Julie with him and, as he grew to know the Hermit better, he no longer worried about us spending the whole evenings down the valley so long as our cycles were in good order. The Hermit was eccentric, Dad said, but no more and, although he might not realise it, we were a blessing to him, a Godsend. We took him out of himself, poor devil.

"He must have been a handsome bloke once," Dad told Mum. "He's got a fine strong nose—it's not a weak face. But he's kind of shrivelled somehow, like a plant that doesn't get enough sun and water. He *creeps*. There's been a tragedy somewhere."

But at that time Sophie and I dismissed that tragedy for

77

fear that if we acknowledged it our happiness might be marred.

As the nights drew out and the sun climbed higher each day at noon we stayed with Caesar later after school, and then rose early the next day to do our neglected homework. We polished and cleaned the tack until it was supple and the bit, buckles and stirrups winked in the sunlight. And we polished and praised Caesar, so that he seemed to grow bigger and prouder day by day, with a new and bolder light in his eye.

Soon we put jumps in the ring, a whole course with wall, and brush, double and triple bars, still allowing him to stop after each one for a lump of sugar; and then Chris and Jane Langton brought their ponies, too, and we made a collecting ring and had a rehearsal. Dad borrowed a microphone from a friend and acted as steward. The Hermit stood as judge in the middle, rather shy and nervous with his hands fluttering again and a grim rather tortoise-like look on his face. We took Caesar in first before he could recall his earlier days and rebel, and he went right round only stopping after every other fence. We kept the jumps down to three feet six and Mustard and Cress who were both just under fourteen hands each jumped a clear round.

"Jump off?" asked Chris.

"No, thank you. Caesar must never be soured," said the Hermit firmly.

After this Chris and Jane came most Saturdays to ride in the field with us, and the Hermit grew interested in them and their riding, although he was too shy or uncertain to instruct them. Sometimes Julie came with Dad and clapped her little hands whenever Caesar jumped a clear round. We gave her rides on his back, her feet in the leathers, our arms holding her in place. Although so far above ground, she was never nervous.

Meanwhile, our talking and gossiping had done great harm, for our stories had been passed from voice to voice and somewhere they had been overheard by evil men eager for gain. One wet evening as we stood cleaning tack in the Hermit's shabby kitchen, the light grey at the window and the thrush's last song stealing across the sodden garden, the door slid open. A man with a stocking over his face sprang into the room, dark eyes gleaming through the nylon. Sophie gasped; her hand flew up to her mouth to stifle a scream; her face, usually so golden, turning to chalk; her eyes were wide, then her body slid slowly to the ground like a puppet whose strings have been cut in the middle of an act. My stomach was a knot; my heart an engine pounding on a hill, and yet I was frozen to the spot; I could not move. Katie ran forward then, barking wildly, smelling evil, white teeth snapping, but was met by the man's boot, a fancy boot with zips, a dusty brown. And then without conscious thought, surprising myself, I threw the bar of saddle soap at the stockinged face; it missed. And I yelled for help, "Thief, Murderer," although what help I expected I do not know. Katie went for the man again and received a second kick right in her face and left then, squealing with pain. Sophie came to life, a dazed expression on her face, as though coming from a dream.

It was all so quick, so sudden and unexpected that it is difficult to remember the order of things. I know the knocking of my knees coincided with the arrival of two other men, and that at the same time I picked up a chair and held it in front of me, and my voice, strange even to my own ears, said, "Go away. Go away. Don't hurt anyone." And then the Hermit's rather querulous voice asked what the uproar was for, and I shouted, "Thieves, run. Hide!" And Sophie made a dive for the door but was caught in a man's arms, and another man came for me, and, although I hit him with the chair, he overpowered me, his beery breath all about my face, and tied me to a chair with a gag of old rags in my mouth. For a minute I thought I would choke, then I got back my breath, and saw that Sophie was also gagged and tied to a wheel-back kitchen chair. The men had disappeared to another part of the house. Were they murderers or thieves? What did they want from the Hermit? The kitchen door was shut. For a short while there was silence while we struggled with our bonds. Then we heard an occasional shout and a cry which could have come from the Hermit or even brave Katie. It was a nightmare which seemed to go on and on. We were both shaking; we watched ourselves shaking with surprise and horror, our bodies seemed to be reacting without our minds; we had no control over them. Yet this was exactly the sort of scene we had seen again and again in television programmes; a scene we accepted as part of every day life so long as we were not part of it.

It was terrible sitting there gagged and not knowing what was happening to the Hermit and Caesar. We had heard so much on the radio news about torture in far away places that our minds quickly conjured up all sorts of horrors and our stomachs clenched. Of course we tried to free ourselves making ridiculous noises through the filthy rags in our mouths which tasted disgustingly of oil. Fright had enfeebled us so much that for a few moments we could not remember where the Hermit kept his kitchen knives; then I walked myself over to the back door taking my chair with me and rubbed the cords round my wrists against the large old-fashioned key in the lock. The cord began to fray. My wrists hurt; at times they felt on fire, but I went on, and suddenly the cord gave way and my hands were free. I pulled off my gag.

"Where are the knives?"

But poor Sophie only made a choking noise. Then I

remembered—in the scullery. I jumped my chair there, opened the drawer in the table by the old-fashioned stone sink and took out a short sharp steel knife. I freed myself then Sophie.

"I want to be sick," my sister said, "that oily taste!"

The shouts upstairs had grown both in volume and frequency.

"Slash open the mattress, he may keep it there."

"Give the guy a kick, man!"

We guessed that the men supposed the Hermit to be a miser with a secret hoard of money.

"We must go for help. We can't tackle them," I whispered. We peered out through the back door. It was pouring with rain and very dark for June. The sky was like a grey desert, with patches of diesel oil, but the garden was ablaze with light for the burglars had switched on many lights. One of the men was now coming out of a side door carrying a plastic bag which appeared to be full of silver or metal objects, another followed with the picture of the labrador dog gazing up at the man with a gun. Both men were of middling height, wearing dark trousers and sweaters and those awful stocking masks. They looked very sinister; perhaps this was their intention. They loaded the plastic bag and the picture into a van, which they had parked near the barn. When they had returned to the house, I said: "Now. We'll get our cycles. Come on, run!"

They were still leaning up against the barn but their tyres were slashed.

"They're taking no chances," I whispered.

"Caesar," hissed Sophie. "The headcollar. Bags me go."

He was standing under the elderberry and fortunately gave only a soft whinny of welcome.

"Will you stay and spy?"

"All right."

I gave her a leg-up, my heart pounding. We could have

ridden one behind the other like lovers of old galloping to Gretna Green to be married by a blacksmith, but I saw the logic of her suggestion, and when the man left the Hermit might need help. It was right that I, the eldest should play the more dangerous part.

I opened the gate and then Caesar's steel-shod feet broke the stillness of the night, loud and clear on the hard surface of the lane.

I threw myself down by the thorn hedge just in time for the next minute a window was opened wide, and a few moments later two men came out in the dusk.

"They'll raise the alarm," one said.

"There was only the girl on the horse. I saw quite clearly," the other said. "If only the old devil would tell us where it is."

"The boy's probably run off. How near is the nearest house?"

"Over a mile."

"We've got a few minutes then."

"Yeah."

Luckily, I was wearing a green sweater and brown corduroys which merged with the ground. I lay in the grass against the hedge. It was very wet. I sank into the grass and the water oozed up and soaked me, and the rain beat mercilessly on my back, while overhead a stuttering aircraft bore its way through the murky sky. Now the hoof beats had faded and gone. The lane was very quiet; even the birds and the cows farther up the valley were silent. The men went back into the house bent on getting all they could before Sophie raised the alarm. She wouldn't be long, I thought, she had been cantering. I could tell by the hoof beats. The men hurried to and fro from the house to the van, while I hardly dared to breathe. I could tell by their voices that they were put out by Sophie's departure; they swore dreadfully and snapped at one another and slammed doors. My heart thumped so noisily that I was sure they would find me and then what would they do? All sorts of horrors came into my mind. I sweated; beads of sweat rose on my forehead and trickled down my face. Then the rain came faster, beating a tattoo on the windows and the rooftops, gurgling in the gutters, hissing as it met a gust of the rising wind. It was a wild night for June. The broken gate, left open, started to swing to and fro, banging and creaking, and I breathed more freely. In the house Katie set up a loud yapping and I feared for the Hermit's life. Were they enemies from whom he had been hiding all these years or were they simply thieves? I started to pray: "Oh God, save the Hermit. God keep him safe. Make these men leave this place and go away. Help us, God!" I must have mouthed this cry for Divine Help, for I took a mouthful of wet grass and earth and nearly died trying not to cough.

After what seemed to me in my cramped condition like an age, but was probably only a minute or two, all the lights of the house went out and the men moved swiftly on their soft soled feet to the van. I heard it start, the quick purr then roar of the engine as they revved her up; then the crunch of the tyres as they met the hard surface of the lane. The van must have gone in the direction of the Langtons for I did not hear it pass me, but the sky had darkened again and the men were driving without lights.

I scrambled to my feet, stiff, sweating yet cold, and went warily to the house. I switched on the kitchen light and saw the intruders' footprints all over the wet brick floor. Avoiding these I entered the passage beyond, which was dark even on the sunniest days, and called:

"Hi, anyone there? Katie, Katie! It's me, Matthew. It's okay. They've gone. You can come out. It's okay, it's okay." My voice sounded a bit strained, pitched a note higher than usually and I was digging my fingernails into the palms of my hand.

"Katie, Katie! Mr. Piers! It's me, Matthew!"

It was no use. Nobody was going to answer. The house seemed horribly dead. But I had to go on. I couldn't stand still. The man and dog might be dying or something. I forced myself up the stairs, my stomach back in a knot, and everywhere I was met by black silence I was afraid of what I might find. More of this than the men, who after all, had gone. I had seen them go. Surely they would not come back.

Supposing the Hermit's head was bashed in; there was blood everywhere, but he was alive? I wouldn't know what to do. Even the thought of the blood made my stomach rise until I thought I should vomit, I turned on each light in each room before entering. Each room was empty and ransacked. There were more bedrooms than I had imagined. They smelt dusty and unused, sort of dead places. I hardly took in the furniture, which was mostly dark and old, or the colour of the walls. I looked under the beds and in the cupboards, and I called out again and again, "Anybody there?" for my voice was better than silence, even though it sounded so thin and hopeless, rather like a cry at sea drowned by the great roar of the waves.

At last in a cupboard I found little Katie crouched in a corner, her face smudged with blood. I picked her up, hugged her to me, comforted by the warmth of her body. Now I wasn't alone any more. The blood on her face was around the mouth, so that it looked as though she had been guzzling tomato ketchup. Only her gums were bleeding now, but one tooth was loose and hanging as though by a thread, kicked from its socket, and one eloquent eye was half closed where the man's boot had landed. I wrapped her in the coverlet on what I supposed was the

Hermit's bed, for it was the only one made-up for use, and left her looking very pathetic, battered and cock-eyed. But where was the Hermit? Had the burglars taken him in the van? There had been no sound of a man being carried against his will across the garden. Perhaps he was dead. Perhaps drugged. Perhaps he had been a spy in the war. A man who killed silently for his country, and these men had come to revenge the death of their fathers by his skilled and merciless hand. All sorts of ridiculous fantasies now ran through my mind. Could he have been in one of the black plastic bags carried so roughly to the van? No, he was too large and I would have seen his feet or his face's whiteness shining through the rain and the grey light of the too-early dusk.

"If only you could speak!" I cried to Katie. "Where is he? What did they do?" I clasped her to me again, glad to feel the warmth of a living thing in this dead, forsaken place.

A moment later, daring to look out of the bedroom window I saw the lights of the police Jaguar sweeping the murky lane. They had been put on full beam, probably because of the rain. Soon two men in uniform were coming through the garden gate. I pushed open the window; looking down I advised them to be careful because there were some fine footprints on the kitchen floor.

"At least you will know the size of their boots," I called.

I marvelled then at the calmness of my voice, which had dropped now to its usual pitch. Suddenly I felt as one must feel after a long and terrible journey when one sees the lights of home shining across the darkness. I felt as though friendly arms were all about me, and the long nightmare was over. This was the dawn. I went down into the kitchen and hopping over the clearest footprints put the kettle on for tea.

"The Hermit's gone," I said. "I've searched. He's not here, not anywhere. I've looked in every cupboard, every chest, under every bed. I've looked, I've looked, I've looked in . . ." I stopped. My voice was taking over control. The friendly arms feeling had gone.

"Steady, son. Sit down, take it easy."

They were very kind, these two young policemen. One of them pulled out a chair for me. "A rough night," he said.

"I'm all right," I told them, thinking of the Hermit. If he was to be saved no time must be lost. "Listen, they drove off in a grey van, but I never took the number. Oh, I wish I had taken the number. Down that way," I waved rather wildly. "With no lights. There were three of them. It was quite a big van, quite big, big enough to take a small amount of furniture, but not a removal van."

"We've put a road block at the end," a policeman said, "but they may have beaten us to it. Now you sit quiet until your Dad comes."

The policemen went upstairs. I could hear their feet on the stairs. For a moment I was alone, and the awful thoughts about the Hermit's fate crowded my mind and made me sweat. I had watched too much violence on television. In a way acts of violence were every day events. In another way they were not. I shut my eyes, but visions of a tortured Hermit were still there. I wanted to be sick. Then Dad arrived and two plain-clothed detectives. Suddenly the Hermit's house had become a scene in "Softly Softly" or "Z Cars."

"Want to come home, Matthew?" asked Dad putting a hand on my shoulder and looking deep into my face. "All right, are you?"

It was good to have him there, so large and calm.

"A bit shaky when we came in," a young policeman said.

He had measured the footprints before going upstairs, now he was putting dust down for fingerprints.

"They wore gloves, black, I think," I said.

"Thanks, son."

The kettle was boiling. I got up and made tea, for if we found the Hermit, I thought he would be suffering from shock.

"I don't want to go home till we've found him," I said.

"But you're soaked."

"I don't care, Dad."

"He's not anywhere in the house," announced the youngest constable coming down the stairs. "There's a little dog on the bed."

"That's Katie."

"Put up a fight, did she?"

"Yes."

I poured tea into the chipped kitchen cups, which the Hermit had bought at Woolworths before the War, and left everyone to help himself to sugar and powdered milk. The rain outside was stopping; the gurgle in the gutters had turned into no more than a grumble and then a gentle drip-drip. But the sky was darkening now with the coming of the night.

"Anyone got a torch?" I asked.

"What for?"

"To look for the Hermit. He may be outside. He could be dy . . . well, you know, loss of blood and all that."

"I've got one," said Dad. "But you drink up your tea first. You're the one suffering from shock. Your teeth were chattering when I came in. Didn't you know? Come on now, drink up." He handed me a cup. "Sophie wanted to stay home. She's had enough."

"And Caesar?"

"He's trampling all over the garden, having the whale

of a time. Oh well, it's an ill wind that blows nobody any good."

The tea made me feel better in spite of the powdered milk taste. Dad fetched his torch from the car. It was an expensive one with a switch so that you could have a long or short beam.

"Don't go into the yard by the barn," said a policeman in a peaked cap. "We've got to measure the tyre marks. I'm glad the rain's laid off. We shall need statements from you children, but they can wait until morning."

We found the Hermit in the front garden, the part Sophie and I never entered. He was bound and gagged and had been literally thrown into a clump of bushes. He was very wet. His face was the colour of putty and his eyes shone feverishly like wet pebbles pushed deep into white sand. And he was trembling. We untied the gag, loosened the cord on his wrists, stood him up. "They took my Landseer, that was my father's. He bought it before the war. Where's Katie? She put up a fight?"

"She's all right. She's on your bed, battered but alive," I said. "They took some silver, too, and the picture with the labrador."

"That was the Landseer . . ." His teeth were chattering. He was in poor shape. Dad picked him up like a child and carried him indoors, and I was glad then that Dad was so strong, so steady, a rock in a storm, to which one could cling.

We cut the Hermit's bonds and gave him tea. The police crowded round him, but the inspector in the peaked cap sent most of them away and fetched one of the plainclothes men.

The Hermit drank his tea obediently, like a young child. He had a hurt and hunted look; his hands were unsteady and his jaw was swelling before our eyes. He seemed to have shrunk; presently he sicked-up his tea, and the inspector sent for an ambulance through his car radio.

"Not fit to make a statement in his present state. Has been kicked around too much," said the detective regretfully. "Best to get him to hospital as soon as we can, might be internal injuries."

The Hermit's clothes were torn and through one tear I could see a purple bruise right across his ribs. It made me feel a little sick. Now he limped away into a corner and sat down with his back to us. After a while he said, "I don't want to go to hospital. I want to stay here. And where's my little dog?"

I went upstairs and fetched Katie, carrying her down in my arms.

"Here's the heroine," I said.

"Poor old lady," said the Hermit.

And then he swore. After that he started to cough and no one seemed able to stop him until the ambulance came, and then he pulled himself together, refused the use of a stretcher or wheel chair, and walked to it absolutely upright. Inside, the ambulance man made him lie down and his last words were,

"Look after the little dog and keep schooling the horse," and then he made a thumbs-up sign before sinking back on the pillows, like a bird beaten by a storm, and closed his eyes.

"Now, Dad, we must take Katie to Mr. Sizer. She may have internal injuries," I said, "and besides—that tooth needs seeing to."

"We'll call in at home on the way and bring your mother up-to-date," said Dad. "Sure you're feeling all right?"

"Fine, thanks."

It was true. Now that the Hermit had gone, that I had seen him, I felt much better and the sick feeling had disappeared.

CHAPTER SIX

"Caesar was fabulous," Sophie said. "He went like the wind. He seemed to understand. He never slipped once or stumbled and he put on a spurt over the bridge. Oh, he's a great horse. But how did you get on?"

I tried to tell her but I couldn't find words for it all. I skipped the more frightening bits; the water oozing in the ditch, the terror of those empty silent rooms, the Hermit's putty white face and the purple bruises I had seen like smudged blackberry juice through the tear in his old grey sweater.

In the middle of a broken night I remembered describing the Landseer to somebody in a shop; the mournful eyes of the faithful labrador, the black of the gun's barrel which seemed to match the dog's coat.

"It's fantastic. I suppose it might be a masterpiece. The Hermit said it could be worth thousands."

"Never!" the now faceless person had retorted. "I just don't believe it!"

And then Sophie had joined in:

"You should see his silver teapot. He never uses it of course. Georgian, he says, ever so old. And there's a milk jug and sugar bowl, a whole set. They're antiques I suppose."

I tried now, in the still watches of the night, to recall the face, but here my mind was a blank. Then I remembered we were in the village's little supermarket, waiting with our wire basket in the inevitable queue. We had been sent down there by our Mum with a shopping list. There were several faces behind us and in front of us; more than one pair of ears must have overheard our remarks. I blushed now with shame.

It was at breakfast the next day that Dad had rather cruelly said we were bird brained.

"You kids have been talking again, haven't you? Boasting about your friendship with a rich old man. Someone must have overheard you."

Sophie burst into tears.

"It's all our fault," she cried. "And now the Hermit may die and then we shall be murderers."

"Now you're going from one extreme to the other," Dad said. "You're exaggerating again."

Dad often had the breakfast blues. If he had any complaint against us it usually came out as he started his cereal. You had to accept that. It was no use grumbling, you just remembered that he felt less angry once he had reached the toast stage. I made a face at Sophie which was meant to mean, cheer up; it's not as bad as all that. But Dad misread the message.

"It's nothing to smile about, Matthew. You should both be thoroughly ashamed of yourselves," he raised his voice. "I do hate smirking," he added.

"O quiet, please!" said Mum, "you'll wake James. And Steve, don't be hard on Matthew and Sophie. They've been through quite an ordeal, and they never meant any harm."

"Fair enough," replied Dad, "I'll shut my trap, but I had to make my point. It isn't as though we hadn't told them before not to gossip about the old man, is it?"

Sophie's tears fell thick and fast on her Ready-Brek and my cornflakes seemed to taste of soap, and then our doleful thoughts were interrupted by Caesar's anxious neigh, and we remembered that we must take him back right away.

The garden was in a dreadful mess, and I was surprised that Dad had not reproached us about this. The lawn was pitted with hoofmarks, the wallflowers were broken and young apples had been knocked or pulled from trees.

We put the headcollar on Caesar and took it in turns to ride him down the lane. It was Thursday and we had been allowed a day off school because the police wanted to take statements from us at eleven o'clock.

After the storm the valley smelt sweet and green: beads of rain shone on the grass in the early sun. Clouds spun lazily in a clear sky like little boats, white sailed, on a calm blue sea. For a moment I felt like singing; then, remembering the Hermit's plight, I sank into gloom.

Kate was still at Frinkley because the vet had decided to keep her under observation for a couple of days in case she was hurt inside. The uprooted tooth he had pulled with a pair of small pliers. Then he had given her a shot of penicillin—to be on the safe side he had said. He had asked whether the old man was badly hurt. "A strange fellow," he had added.

Dad had telephoned the hospital first thing in the morning to ask after the Hermit and had been told his condition was "quite satisfactory." Now suddenly everything seemed rather flat after all the tension of yesterday evening. I think Sophie and I both felt a little like punctured balloons and we could think of nothing better to do than look back on our past behaviour with remorse.

Dad had been a boy during the war and he had told us of the posters put on the billboards of that time, declaring that careless talk costs lives. No one was supposed to gossip about troop movements or airports or the positioning of anti-aircraft guns, because such information might be useful to the enemy. Lots of things, Dad said, were hush hush. Everyone had had to learn to curb his tongue. Now travelling slowly down that sunlit lane the billboard phrase plagued my mind and somehow pin-pointed my own carelessness.

"At least we haven't *only* done the Hermit harm, I mean we have done him good, too. We have brought him out into the sunshine and put him in touch with the modern world through the 'Telegraph'," said Sophie.

"I didn't realise that picture was a Landseer."

"Just as well or we might have given that vital fact away also."

"Oh shut up. You talked about the Georgian silver remember? I thought it was just tarnished metal."

"I know."

"It's no good crying over spilt milk."

"No."

The Hermit's place seemed strange without him and we missed Katie's welcoming face. We didn't stay long and were home by ten o'clock.

The detective who came to see us was small for a policeman, but very wiry with a leathery face and a way of staring you in the eyes until you felt uncomfortable. I did not enjoy my interview with him as much as I had hoped. In the course of it I found that I had noted very little of use during the burglary and I was a poor witness when it came to describing men's voices. Once again I wished that I had taken the number of the van.

"Schoolboys usually do that as a matter of course," the detective said, tapping our dining room table with his biro pen.

"I am rather vague. I mean as a person. I'm sorry."

"Can't you remember anything else that might identify them. Come on, think."

"Beery breath," I said suddenly. "The one who tied me up smelled of beer."

"Now we are getting somewhere. We'll check the local pubs," the detective said.

Sophie fared no better.

"They were wearing stockings," she said, over and over

93

again, and then was quite unable to answer the questions about denier.

"Sort of neither very fine nor very coarse, sort of middling."

Dad had fetched Katie from the vet's place the next evening, but of course she could not stay with us because of James's allergies. So we took her down to the Hermit's house and Dad drove down each morning to give her a run and a bowl of milk, and after school she was with us and Caesar out in the field as usual. Mr. Perks seemed to have brought the Hermit fifty tins of dog meat which we supposed must have been a bargain offer, so there was no problem about Katie's meals.

Every newspaper we saw seemed to have printed a piece on the Hermit's burglary, partly, we decided, because newspaper editors know that British readers are fascinated by any news concerning a recluse, and partly because of the Landseer. One ambitious newspaper reporter managed to get into Frinkley Hospital with a small camera hidden under his coat and photographed the Hermit sitting up in bed looking weird and bird-like. Three reporters called at our home in the hope of getting "a story" from us; thinking we would be short of money because of the strike they offered us cash if we would talk. But Dad forbade it. On no account, he said, were we to accept money or gain publicity through the Hermit's misfortune.

"Just a few words," we pleaded, wanting to see ourselves quoted in the newspapers. "After all we *were* there." But he said, principles were principles and he was sticking by his, and he sent away all the reporters and set himself to mending our cycles which he soon put in order again.

Katie's picture appeared in the local evening paper the day after the Hermit's. She had been snapped at the vet's place after a newspaper photographer had made friends with one of the veterinary nurses. She looked so pathetic and sweet with her swollen eyelid that an old lady sent her a giant box of choc-drops addressed to the vet's surgery.

Three days after the burglary, on a Sunday, we were allowed to visit the Hermit in hospital, taking with us the pile of letters which had landed so unexpectedly on his doorstep. He greeted us very calmly, his beaky face quite tranquil, his eyes empty of emotion, and his thin hands lying still on the white bed cover as though they were made of plastic and did not really belong to him. There was a smell of antiseptic and an air of stark cleanliness which made me feel out of place.

Dad fetched an empty chair from across the ward and we all three sat down.

"How's Caesar and my little old lady, Madame Katie?" asked the Hermit in a slow careful voice, as though he wanted each word to come out perfectly all on its own, not run into another, but beautifully rounded.

We brought him up-to-date and after thanking us for all our trouble, he said, "Keep schooling, keep at it, plenty of road work. This won't stop us doing a clear round at the show. You're to be the rider, Matthew, because you're the eldest and your legs are longer than Sophie's. He's a big horse, a great horse, very like one my father used to ride long before the last war called Big Ben—same black points and kind head. I'm sure my sister noticed the similarity."

"She wanted to melt your heart. She knows you well," Dad said, grinning his big-dog grin. "How's life here? Getting bored, are you?"

The Hermit smiled in a ghostly sort of way.

"Nurses are very kind, delightful girls all of them, nothing too much trouble for them and well spoken, I like that. And the doctors? The junior registrar seems very young, no more than a boy really, but I suppose he knows his job; he's got a lot of responsibility. Then there's an Indian, a fine fellow, very sensitive face he has, walks upright, square shouldered, but he has rather poor English, which makes things difficult. The specialist is a different kettle of fish altogether, of course, an older man, trained in Scotland, he told me; soft spoken and much admired. Sister is in quite a tizzy when he's due to make a round. We've all got to look our best then."

"Well, after being here you won't want to be a recluse any longer. You'll be renting yourself television and all, I expect," ventured Dad, looking incredibly heavy and strong like a well fed mastiff beside a diseased saluki. "I mean you've got used to life outside now, haven't you?"

"*Do* make it colour T.V. It's much better for the wild-life programmes," I put in quickly.

The Hermit seemed to shrink back into himself. We had said the wrong thing, upset him.

"It's very quiet here, plenty of rules so that nobody intrudes. The nurses treat us like children. They tuck us up; we're protected. That's nice when you're ill and very appropriate, but it's not like the world outside, is it?"

"No offence meant," said Dad quickly.

"None taken."

"Look," cried Sophie, wanting to break down the barrier which seemed to be growing taller between the two men. "Look at all these letters we found on your door mat. Fabulous! Do you think they are from well-wishers or friends who have lost touch with you? Some have come quite a long way. See, there's one from Poole, Dorset, and another from Cumberland.

Sophie, who has a horrible and so far incurable habit of reading other people's postmarks, now handed the Hermit his mail which she had secured with a rubber band. "Frightfully exciting," she added.

"*Frightfully* not *frightfully*, surely," said Dad.

"You know what I mean," replied Sophie, looking into the Hermit's face.

"I'm not going to use that awful phrase which came in just after the war—'I couldn't care less'," said the Hermit, "but that is how I feel about all these letters. Maybe I shan't open them. I don't want to get involved. I just want to be left alone. There might be something in one of them which might upset my peace of mind. It is all most unfortunate and uncalled-for."

He looked tiresomely petulant and Sophie said, "Oh no, Mr. Hermit, you can't leave them unopened, that would be most unkind and selfish, too, and so disappointing for the people who sent them. I bet some of them are *Get well* cards, pictures of horses or something."

I hated her bossiness. Why couldn't she let the poor man do as he wanted? I guessed that she longed to see some of the letters herself, to arrange the get well cards on his locker in front of the bunch of carnations sent by the local paper in exchange for the photograph they had taken without permission—a sort of peace offering.

"Now, Sophie, you're talking to me as though I am a child, and that won't do," said the Hermit patiently, "and I'm just old enough to be your grandfather. I'm fifty-four."

He looked so much older at this time that we were all lost for words, then Dad said,

"Much wrong with you, Mr. Piers? Did they knock you about? Any bones broken?"

"Cracked ribs, cracked jaw, multiple bruises, shock. Soon be out. I've had worse before."

"May we tidy your house? Someone ought to do it. Those men left an awful mess. All the drawers have been tipped out."

"The police said they would do it. Thank you all the

D

same, Sophie, for your kind offer," replied the Hermit. Then he turned his face to Dad looking for all the world like some bedraggled old bantam cock about to declare war on a full grown rooster.

"Now don't you start trying to drag me back into everyday life. I like my own company and I like peace and quiet in my own home. I've no wish to enter the hurly burly again. The civilised world has gone mad anyway. It worships the motor car, the machine, and everyone is running so fast collecting filthy lucre that they cannot pause to contemplate or enjoy life. *What is this life, if full of care, we have no time to stand and stare.*"

"I don't agree with you," replied Dad solemnly. "I think you paint too gloomy a picture by half. These nurses here are not chasing after money. But let's agree to differ. I don't want an argument."

After this we ran out of topics of conversation. Dad offered to bring the Hermit books or magazines or newspapers and what about cash? Had he any change? The Hermit said Mr Perks had come in, the kind soul, bless him, and had cashed a cheque.

"The only thing I always carry in my hip pocket is a cheque book," confessed the Hermit. "I am in need of nothing, thank you. I'm happy to doze the days away."

We presented him with After Eight chocolates, grapes and lime juice, which Dad had bought for us to bring, for which he thanked us politely but with little enthusiasm. Dad said the Hermit was tired and we rose to go. Now for the first time I was conscious of all the other patients, most of them sitting up, trying to be polite and cheerful to their visitors. The beds were iron, high and white; the walls were cream with apple green woodwork, rather like an old fashioned dairy; the floors highly polished, covered in plain blue linoleum. It was all a bit stark, although orange curtains lent at least a little warmth, and there were loads of summer flowers on lockers and the centre table. The Hermit's sister had sent him yellow roses.

"Would you like us to come again?" asked Dad, as we turned to go.

"No really, it's very kind of you to offer. I appreciate it. But I shall be out soon. Those chocolates will build me up, put a bit of flesh on the old bones. Face looks a bit like a vulture's doesn't it? The little fair nurse holds a looking glass in front of me while she does my hair, so I can't help but see myself—bit of a shock really. I mean shaving at home I only looked at my chin and cheeks, kept my eyes off the rest . . ."

"Vultures are predators. You could never look like a predator, Mr. Piers," said Dad firmly.

"You're fabulous, and we all love you," said Sophie.

"When they showed me my picture in the paper I wanted to throw in the sponge altogether, and I nearly threw those carnations through the window, so they stuck a needle in my arm to calm me down—after fetching the junior registrar for advice. You can't win here. We are like animals in a zoo. There's always the traquillising dart by way of an injection. I'm not grumbling mind you. A prick in the arm is better than a crack on the head and no food for a week. I've tried them both."

We walked back down the ward watched by some of the patients, to whom no doubt the Hermit was something of a curiosity. I tried not to stare back. Apart from manners, I did not want to see anything which might upset me. But from the corner of my eye I saw a red-faced man with one leg suspended in the air on a sort of pulley, and a boy of about fifteen patiently knitting what appeared to be a dish cloth.

We were glad to leave the smell of surgical spirit and disinfectant behind us.

In the street, Sophie said, "He spoke so carefully and

slowly. It was odd. He didn't seem like *our* Hermit. He's changed."

"He's on drugs, pain killers, I expect," said Dad, "and he's probably still suffering from shock. Shock slows speech. Those thugs kicked him around. A spell in hospital will do him good, poor old chap."

Then Dad swore and we all made our way to the car park.

CHAPTER SEVEN

LOOKING back now over the years, I realise that after the burglary my character changed a little and I took a leap forward in my work. Subjects previously dull became interesting, and teachers I had disliked seemed not so stupid after all. The Careers Master began to consider my future more seriously and O Levels became an exciting challenge rather than a depressing obstacle looming tiresomely in the future. I started to ration my television viewing so that I could pay more attention to my homework. I borrowed books from the library by Alistàir Maclean and John Buchan. I wrote an essay on Disraeli which was highly praised by the history master and for the first time in my life, a piece I wrote for the school magazine was printed. In short I became both hopeful and ambitious, emerging it seemed from a fog into a clear and easy world.

My riding, too, appeared to take a turn for the better. Caesar was angelic; he jumped magnificently. One evening he cleared four feet six with me and he jumped many a clear round over the courses we made from old oil cans and poles as well as Dad's fences. We were, of course, careful never to tire him, asking no more than a few jumps each day, and then taking him for a hack. I fell off again when he shied at a piece of fluttering paper just after clearing a three feet double. I fell on my tummy and the air came out of me in a groan that I could not control, for all at once my body seemed to have a life of its own. Sophie was alarmed. Running across the field in leaps and bounds like a startled hare, she called my name over and over again. But I was only winded and once the groan was out I was little more than shaken and remounted straight away to prove to myself that I was not afraid.

Three days after our visit the Hermit came home because the hospital needed his bed for another patient. In the fitful sunlight he looked frail and white, like an insect that has crept out from under a stone after a long winter. He obstinately refused the services of the Home Help the hospital recommended and the Council wished to provide for him.

"No busy-bodies. All nosey parkers OUT," he said. He crept back into his house, which had been well tidied by two constables and dusted by Sophie and me. We had put a great vase of flowers on the table and a banner saying WELCOME above the front door, but he seemed oblivious to these niceties. Only Katie with her wagging tail and her wild delight brought a smile to the man's grim face. We made him tea, which Sophie poured out, and produced chocolate wholemeal biscuits and bullseyes. We talked brightly like mothers do when they take their children out from boarding school for an afternoon. But it was stilted and false and we knew then that it would be a while before the Hermit could be as he was before the burglary.

A little earlier I had made a new friend at school, John Heywood, a fair, freckled, thoughtful boy who cared little for pop stars or footballers. A new pupil, for his father had only recently bought a junk shop in the district, he had decided already that he wished to be a librarian as he was very interested in books. He found it hard to keep his eyes away from the written word and had rather an irritating habit of reading aloud anything printed, be it no more than the letters on a shop front or the advertisement on the side of a bus.

There was a custom at school among some of the boys to meet at a coffee bar called the Roma Cafe on the way home. There they would smoke cigarettes, drink coffee, hot chocolate topped with foaming cream, or coke and try to appear sophisticated. The boys usually sat on high stools at the bar, unless they were meeting a girl when they would move off to one of the corner tables, each of which was romantically lit by a small lamp with a red pleated shade.

I had not been to the Roma Cafe since Caesar had come into my life. Now, after school two days before my birthday and the day after the Hermit's return from hospital, John said, "What's the hurry? Forget the horse for a moment. Let's go for a quick one round the corner." And I agreed.

The place was already full of cigarette smoke when we arrived and all the stools were occupied by fifteen year olds, who were making a good deal of noise mimicking a new teacher who spoke with a broad Yorkshire accent.

"What are you going to have? This is on me," said John, just as though we were grown-ups in a pub.

"A capuchino," I said, trying to appear well-travelled, having learned this little bit of Italian from a friend who picked up foreign languages very quickly.

We moved over to a central table, leaving the corner ones for the boys with girls, and sat down.

"What do you think about Monte Carlo going?" I asked.

"Montgomery?"

"Yes, haven't you learned the jingo yet?"

"He's biology, isn't he?"

"Known by some unkindly people as 'Goofy'. He's a sort of elderly edition of Ken Dodd. They say he's had an heart attack."

"Who's they?"

"Those in the know—Hugh and Robert, for example. Bad luck for him."

"Depends who we get in his place."

"They say it will only be a temporary, just to tide us over to the new school year."

We started to talk about the Hermit's return from hospital then, but I had not got very far before we were joined by a man and a woman, who sat down on the other side of the table. Remembering that fearful warning 'Careless talk costs lives' I fell silent.

"Go on," urged John. "What happened then?"

"Not here. Later." I tried to make the right sort of grimace to indicate that I could not talk of the Hermit in front of the newcomers at our table. The man fascinated me. In some strange way he was familiar. But where had I met him? He was of medium height with a fresh complexion, a King Charles I moustache and burning dark eyes, the sort of eyes I thought you might see in the face of a cornered wolf. The woman with him had very short hair cut close to the head, heavily made-up pale blue eyes, a turned-up nose and a teasing expression, which somehow irritated me. I suppose now that I am older I should describe her as coy, but then I could find no word for her. Both the man and the woman were eating fried hamburgers with onions, chips and peas—or rather, to be exact, the girl was picking hers over and the man was wolfing his.

John started to tell me about a film he had seen recently and then about "Jesus Superstar", which was being shot just then, while I watched the man, who, having finished his meal, lit a filter-tip cigarette, which he held between his first finger and his thumb. His hands were, I saw, unusually short, his nails severely bitten so that his finger-tips actually looked sore. They were hands I had seen before, hands that belonged to a moment I had actually experienced. But which moment? The face, too, was not new to me nor the voice. There were parts of a jigsaw which I was trying to put together in my mind, as John went on talking. They were surely the hands that had tied me to the chair in the Hermit's kitchen, for looking back I remembered now that the masked man had removed his black gloves to tie the knots, swearing under his breath, because the cord had been damp and stiff. At the time I was not aware of his hands, not consciously, but my brain must have been. It recorded them, and now it gave me back that moment as a filing clerk might bring out a letter long ago forgotten. And the whole man was familiar because he had been so near me and there had been an aura around him which was here, too.

"You're not listening," complained John. "You're miles away."

"Sorry," as I answered the man looked at me and in his dark eyes I thought I saw a flicker of recognition. He stubbed out his cigarette.

"Come on," he said.

"Let me finish. We've only just come in," said the girl. I started to talk very fast about the sort of man we might find teaching us Natural History the next week. I was sorry for poor old Monte Carlo, but he had been a bore, and he had given us very little work on projects. Somehow we had all needed maths all the time, and maths were my weakest subject, so I felt a failure in the only subject about which I really cared. I felt bitter, because all the time Sophie, who was not especially interested in natural history, was doing the sort of work I wanted to do, and she

104

was only in the first year of her secondary school. My heart was thumping as I talked and the man was scrutinising me while waiting for his girl to finish her plate of food. A waft of beery breath would have made the picture more complete.

"Come on," he said again. "Leave it. You're only picking it over."

He gave the girl a long significant look and jerked his thumb in direction of the door, and at last the message sank home. She rose to her feet without a word and they both left the cafe without looking back.

"In a minute," I said to John, in a low dramatic voice. "We must go to the police."

"The police? You're joking."

"It's no good us following him because he knew me. I'm certain he recognised me." I explained my suspicions.

"But hands," objected John, "lots of people have stumpy hands with bitten nails."

"It's not only the hands, it's a hunch, if you like, a feeling I can't describe; it's uncanny. I suppose everyone has an aura, a sort of atmosphere around them; they give off their own, very own electric waves or something . . . well, that's what I'm talking about."

"People who are attacked are usually very bad at recognising their attackers. That's why identity parades are often such a farce," said John gloomily.

"Come on," I said. "No time for argument. On the trail!"

We found a tall, lean constable at the station; hatless behind a desk, he looked as though he couldn't have knocked a ghost over and even his smile was thin. He said the detective in charge of the case was out just now but would be in touch with us as soon as he was back. He thanked us wanly.

"He's probably been out on patrol all night or something," said John. "Dad used to know a copper who had to resign: the hours were too long. He got a disease called TB. It's a terrible life if you're not strong."

We parted then and I sped home very fast, for I was a little afraid the man with the Charles I moustache might come after me.

We didn't see the Hermit that evening for I was late and Sophie was busy making preparations for his birthday. Caesar no longer needed hay as there was plenty of rich June grass. Sophie had persuaded Mum to make a military pudding for the Hermit's birthday supper the next day. She had found a recipe after searching through several cookery books in the school and public library. Dad went out and bought half a bottle of champagne, which he could not afford, and Sophie and I borrowed from Julie, who had a bulging money box, to buy the Hermit a china horse costing one pound, thirty-five pence, which we hoped would adorn one of the mantelpieces stripped bare by the burglars.

Our Mum was strangely quiet as though there were a problem on her mind, which was odd because James had been quite well for several days, my schoolwork had improved and Julie had become keen on the local playgroup and stopped her tantrums. We thought that perhaps the strike was worrying her. Too shy to ask what the matter was, I helped her tidy the kitchen. We all watched "Dad's Army" on the television and afterwards Sophie played pop records: "Chart Busters Volume VI" because it had "School's Out" and then "Puppy Love". Dad, who hates pop music, said he thought he would go to see how the Hermit was.

"I'll prepare him for his celebration supper tomorrow. We don't want him filling up on Bovril and chocolate wheatmeal biscuits at half-past five."

Mum went to bed with a headache; her clear, golden
106

complexion had turned a dusty white and her blue eyes had the faded look of a sweater left too long to soak in soap powder. She asked Sophie to stop playing records for the night, and Sophie rather horribly said that the house was too small. The Langtons had an attic where they could play pop to their hearts' content and no one complained. It wasn't fair, she declared. Why did we have to live in such a pokey dump? Mum called from her bed that Chris and Jane were spoiled; they would grow up into selfish people because they were not trained to be considerate, to think of others, which was the very basis of good manners. Sophie muttered something unkind under her breath, packed away the records and went upstairs to pin a new picture of her favourite pop singer on her wall.

I had told no one about the detective, because somehow the atmosphere at home had not been right, so they were a bit surprised when he rang early next morning. I had hoped that I would get a day off school to see him, but he said he would talk to me by arrangement in the headmaster's office or some such place, which sounded rather important.

He turned out to be tall and burly with shoulders wide enough to span the average doorway, with a bald pate slightly speckled like an egg, fringed with a neat border of thick grey hair. He looked as though he would make a good rugby centre-forward. Although interested in my hunch he said he was not sure that it would prove to be a "useful lead". It all seemed rather a coincidence. Lots of people bit their finger-nails and nowadays Charles I moustaches were a commonplace. It was very easy to be mistaken. He regretted that I had not told the detective on the scene of the burglary that my assailant had removed his gloves. "It's just possible that we might have got some finger-prints."

He read through the statement I had made the day after the burglary and I must say it sounded pretty feeble.

Unfortunately news of my chat with the detective leaked out and one or two boys made nasty remarks to me about mixing with fuzz—as they called the police. It was all a bit worrying. I just wanted to go home and bury my face in Caesar's coat and forget all about the police and school.

I was glad when the afternoon wore to an end. I sped home with the sun in my eyes and the scent of drying hay in my nostrils and above me a deep blue sky adorned with clouds like spirals of cotton wool dragged from the neck of an aspirin bottle. The summer breeze was warm and soft in my face and I was happy. For a few moments the world seemed at my feet. I thought of the Hermit's party and of riding Caesar again, dear Caesar who was always solid and reliable, who asked no questions and told no lies, but grew more obliging and lovable day by day and yet never lost his dignity.

The Hermit's party went well. We all gobbled up the cold chicken, ham, pork pie, salad, crisp French bread and pickles, as though we had not eaten for days, and then took the military pudding, a suet affair with a white sauce rather more slowly. Sophie and I each drank half a glass of champagne and the Hermit drank the rest. We sang Happy Birthday and drank his health; and then the Hermit sang "Roll Out The Barrel", "I've Got Sixpence" and "Lili Marlene" in a voice which must have been a fine baritone long ago, but was now croaky and uneven. He proposed the health of the visitors, who were, of course, Sophie and I, saying "Santé", I proposed a toast to Katie and Caesar and then all the champagne was finished.

Afterwards we rode Caesar in the field and the Hermit, buoyed up we supposed by the champagne, claimed a turn. We thought his seat a little old-fashioned; his legs a fraction too far forward and his reins too long, but of course we didn't tell him this. He walked Caesar round the field two or three times, then trotted once, reined back three paces, returned to us and dismounted.

"Weak as a willow, no muscles and the heart going bumpety bump, and breath short as a train's steam when there's a rotten firemen on the footplate," complained the Hermit. "I shall be stiff as a board tomorrow, crippled." All the same he was smiling—not twitching, *really* smiling, with a twinkle in his eye and two little red blobs like overgrown cherries on his cheeks.

"It's been a fine birthday and I'm bursting with appreciation. You've been absolutely tophole, prang-on as the chaps in the air force used to say. And don't forget it's your birthday tomorrow, young man." He slapped me jovially on the shoulder. "A grand day," he added.

"No chance of that. Are you sure you *can't* come to the feast? We would all love to have you," I said.

"Yes, do change your mind," urged Sophie. "Come and see where we live for a change. *Do*. It would be great."

"I should fall down, you know I would. I should be the spectre at the feast. It's definitely too far. Now, how goes the enemy?"

"Seven o'clock," I told him, glancing at my watch.

"What about a bit of road work, toughen up Caesar's muscles? Nothing like a bit of road work."

"A headache," said Sophie, passing a hand across her eyes. "You'd best go, Matthew."

"Is it the champagne? Hang on, I'll get you an aspirin, soon put you right. It's not often you're out of sorts," said the Hermit kindly. "You take the horse, Matthew."

As I rode away down the lane, I marvelled at the Hermit's quick recovery, high spirits and kindliness. I wondered whether the pills he had brought back from the

109

hospital helped, whether he had really taken a permanent turn for the better and was going to become more human.

I rode at first on the lane, then turned off by a copse where the river wound its sleepy silver way through the patchwork valley. The corn was still a pale and lovely green but turning to yellow. Dog roses shone like white stars in the hedges. The larks soared swift and light, their nests below deeply hidden; shadows lengthened as the sun slipped down below the wooded slopes, cushioned in clouds of shining gold, leaving a wan moon frail and noiseless in a stone grey sky like a ghost at the end of a party. I loved those Kentish evenings; the nutwoods framed against the horizon, the air sharp suddenly and cool; the strange blue light creeping over the fields before the night came, the dampness and the stillness of it all. I rode back through the fruit farms cantering between regiments of neatly pruned trees, heavy with young apples like green pom-poms.

Back at the Hermit's house I found Dad waiting with the car to run us home. The strike, he said, was over. He would be back at the Mill tomorrow to get the machines working with an extra two pounds a week in his pay packet after tax. He smiled like a good-natured dog as he opened the car door for us to get in. Sophie and I had almost forgotten the strike and we had become accustomed to having Dad around every day, so that, although we said "Fine" and "Great", we didn't really mean it. We were going to miss him and once back at work his nerves would become frayed again and there would be times when we must creep about the house because he was sleeping after the night shift. But at least there would be more money, and our Mum would not have to worry so much about the soaring food prices. Perhaps, I thought, we might now have fewer herrings and more beef. It would be a welcome change. Sophie's mind was on the same tack.

"Do you think we can rise again to éclairs on Sundays?" she asked.

"May be. Better ask your Mum," said Dad.

The next day was my birthday, but I wakened late, which was a sure sign that I was growing old, for in the past I had always wakened at six and spent two agonising hours waiting for the house to come alive.

I did not expect very grand presents because of the strike, and I was not surprised when I found that the riding coat bought for me by my parents was second hand. It had cost three pounds from the Good As New Shop, was made of herringbone tweed and actually looked new. It fitted me well, but in spite of all my efforts, I could not prevent a fleeting expression of disappointment to cross my face. There is quite a big difference between a garment straight off the shop rail and one which has actually been used by someone else, however slightly. Mum didn't miss that momentary disappointment.

"All the new ones were eight pounds or more. You're a big boy now. Look, it's hardly worn anywhere."

"It's smashing," said Dad. "Fits you a treat."

Turning and twisting in front of the looking-glass in my parents' bedroom I felt horribly self conscious. Thank goodness, the brace was coming off my teeth next week. A brace *and* glasses had been a bit much, I thought, rather unfair, when boys like Chris got by without any such awful artificial aids *and* were bright as well!

"I've got you some gloves to go with it," said Dad tossing me a small parcel. They were yellow string ones, the rather expensive kind. Sophie then handed me a long thin package which turned out to be a riding cane. My mother's parents had sent me two pounds to put towards a pair of binoculars. Dad's parents were dead, but he had

111

an unmarried sister, a school teacher, who had sent me another pound and an atlas. She always sent me an educational present; all sorts of reading aids came when I was small, and then encyclopaedias and dictionaries, and now this atlas.

"That will help with your homework, your geography," Mum said.

"You will be able to trace the river Nile," said Sophie with a little mocking smile.

Later, while I gobbled my breakfast, Sophie pushed an envelope from the Hermit in front of my nose.

"Your present, lucky dog."

Inside the envelope was a home-made card with a pound note pinned to it. The card was made from yellowing cartridge paper which the Hermit had tried to clean with bread. On the front he had pasted a picture of a bay hunter with black points cut from some magazine and inside he had written in beautiful copperplate the following verses:

Once We Went Gaily

Once we went gaily with never a care,
And the bigger the fences, the bolder we were
Once the wild wind was our spur and our lash,
Once we would laugh at the splinter and crash
As the rails broke behind us, and thrill to the call
Of twelve foot of water or five feet of wall.

Once we would cope with the bucker's demands,
Once the hard puller came back to our hands;
Once the green four year old, fretting and free,
Flinging the foam in white flecks to his knee,
Bent to our bidding and held us our place,
O'er the stiffest of country whatever the pace.

To blood running hotly to hearts beating strong.
Not the longest of days was a moment too long;
Till the evening drew over its mantle of stars
We would ride to the hoof-beat and rattle of bars.
There was song in the gale; there was kiss in the rain;
Ah! Once we went gaily but never again!

For the harsh years have stolen that magical zest
When with confident courage we rode with the best
Now swift and unchallenged the braver may pass
On their reefing blood horses hard held on the grass;
The nerve is departed, the rapture denied,
And the chase must be left to the young ones to ride.

Will Olgilvie.

I read the poem twice. So he saw me in his place. His nerve had departed. Had he copied out the verses while I rode through the valley in the evening sun after he had tried Caesar, while Sophie nursed her aching head? Was I supposed to be the braver? Did he write them in a moment of sadness? I did not suppose I would ever bring myself to question him so I would have to guess the answers.

"You'll be late for school," our Mum said. "I know it's a special day, but . . ."

Dad had already gone. Sophie seized her satchel.

"Boring old geometry with Snookers," she complained. I ran out leapt on my cycle and sped away, brief case in hand, the sun behind me.

"And the chase must be left to the young ones to ride." It was a rotten poem, but special because the Hermit had sent it as a sort of message, and I liked "Till the evening drew over its mantle of stars," for I loved a night sky. Sometimes I would stand at my window for ages gazing out into the moonlight.

Usually going to school spoils birthdays, but this time it actually improved mine, because it was the day the new biology master came and he took us out at once on a field day. His name was Marcus Davies and he told us that he was half Welsh and half Irish. "A proper Celt," he said, "just back from an expedition in Brazil." Bearded, with dark eyes, sturdy with fine strong hands, he seemed to *care* and he became for us something of a hero. Most important to me at the time, he saw that I also cared; he seemed to take my interest in wildlife into his hands, to mould it, fire it and throw it back to me enhanced.

Twenty of us went out that afternoon to a piece of scrubland owned by a developer. We stood knee deep in wellington boots in a stream, soon to be culverted, collecting specimens in nets for examination in the school lab and samples of water for analysis. I found two water beetles and a shrimp and John fished out two bullheads. Marcus Davies became very excited whenever any one fished out anything and all twenty of us caught his enthusiasm. It was awful to think that in a few months the earth movers would be coming in to level the ground, fell the trees and build tall blocks of flats.

"Boxes for people who don't really want boxes at all," said our new teacher furiously. "Sometimes I would like to see all town planners lined up and shot. Now don't look so shocked, John, I don't really mean it. They do their best. There are people to house, but all the same. . . ."

On the way back to school I fell in beside Marcus Davies, and told him about the goldcrest and the woodpeckers at the Hermit's place and he became quite excited.

"Tell me *exactly* where, show it to me on a map when we get back, will you?"

I told him about Caesar and the voles in the bank and the stoat or weasel we had once seen in the copse behind the house.

114

"But they are *very* rare now. Did you know that? It's fantastic. I shall go there in my old bus. You know I've got a broken down old van? My mother, who's a part-time nurse, drives a little Triumph sports car, but I prefer my broken down machine. I don't want to enter the car status thing. I refuse to worship the combustion engine."

I said I was sure the Hermit would be delighted to see him, for who, I thought, could *not* be pleased to see Marcus Davies?

"I shall bring my binoculars. We shall build a hide. I shall take photographs. I've got a telescopic lens. We might even get them published. Matthew, I'm so glad you've told me about this place. I wish there were more old men like your Hermit who would leave things exactly as they are. We are all getting too tidy. We sweep away rotten logs, cut down undergrowth, throw up our hands in horror at a nettle, and yet all these things provide cover or food for some insect or bird."

Speeding home later, the wind in my face again, I felt as though I had wings. My fate was settled, I was going to be a naturalist. I was going to be a Marcus Davies. Now I would work, yes, I would surprise everyone. The noisy paper mill was not for me.

All at once school had lost its bars; it was no longer a prison; it was a treasure trove.

CHAPTER EIGHT

LIFE is patchy, isn't it? There are times when everything seems to go right and other times when misfortunes seem to dog your steps and black even the sunniest days.

After my birthday the Hermit and I, born under the same star, seemed to hit a good patch, which appeared to me then to go a long way towards proving there was something in this horoscope business after all, although heavens knows why or how. But, perhaps, looking back after several years, I have forgotten all the little irritations, perhaps my mind has kicked out all unhappy and disappointing memories, wanting to preserve at least a few months unblotted by trouble like a clean page perfectly inscribed with some beautiful message or great thought.

July came golden with sunshine. The hay was in, leaving a yellow stubble, the hops were swelling in the valley clambering untidily on their rustic poles. The corn was turning from cool green to gold, while amongst it the first poppies burst into flower like little red flags on a map, and above it the larks sang all day long tirra lirra, tirra lirra, rising and sinking like torn paper. And sometimes in the mornings the heat lay hazy on the landscape, the light above it blue; the trees so still they were like models. Bright butterflies skimmed feather-light in the Hermit's wild aromatic garden. The world seemed sweet with the scents of honeysuckle, warm ripening fruit and mown grass drying in the sun.

It was on such a day that Marcus Davies came with John one Saturday to meet the Hermit. He came with a welcoming smile on his face, wearing old jeans and a torn shirt, binoculars and camera slung over his shoulder.

The Hermit was riding Caesar when he saw the bearded figure at the gate with the fair freckled boy. Had he been on foot he might have fled, but as the Hermit once said himself, astride a horse he was a different man. Perhaps the height gave him a sense of power.

"These are my naturalist friends. Remember I told you? Marcus Davies and John Heywood, whom he has given a lift."

"They have cameras," said the Hermit suspiciously. "Always beware of people with cameras."

"Do you think you could spare them a patch for bird watching?"

I wanted to bring my friends together into one big happy family. Because the three of them appeared to like me I thought they must like each other.

"I don't like publicity. Too many people are coming here, too many faces, too many corners. I don't like it at all. This is my place, not a public park."

My heart seemed to slump down into my feet. The Hermit's face looked quite white and spiteful.

"We will hide right out of your sight," said Marcus Davies in his soft sing-song voice, which was somehow neither Irish nor Welsh but a mixture of the best of both. "We'll be so quiet you won't even know we are here. And I promise we won't use our cameras if you don't want us to. I will put them in my old bus outside."

"I've been beaten up once already. Life has not treated me kindly," said the Hermit riding a little closer on Caesar who was eyeing Marcus's pockets hopefully.

"He's a beauty. Look at that conformation! a splendid front. I should think he's a great ride."

"Do you know something about horses, then?" asked the Hermit, his eyes lighting up. "Are you a rider?"

"I'm a zoologist and botanist. I know a bit about animals. My mother was a rider once—she's Irish—and I rode as a boy. Actually I've been riding mules in Brazil."

"Did she jump banks?"

"Who?"

"Your mother. I've never taken a real bank. You've got to change legs on the top, haven't you? I'm a bit old to start learning now."

"Yes, I'm sure she changed legs—in Cork."

"Used to be a great riding place, Cork."

"But I grew up mostly in Wales," said Marcus. "My father was a hill farmer."

117

"All right," said the Hermit with a wry smile. "Go along with you, hide in that spinney behind the barn and keep that boy you've got with you under control, and don't let me catch sight of you again today. Go on! You look at the dicky birds! And leave the old man in peace."

Was he mocking them? Or was it shyness which made him talk like that? I didn't know and I was a bit embarrassed, but Marcus was smiling and taking the whole thing as a joke.

It was the first of many visits, and gradually Marcus won the Hermit's confidence. He treated him as he would a nervous animal, never approaching him, but waiting for the man's natural curiosity to bring him nearer. By mid July a hide was built in the copse, and the Hermit was there watching too, and secretly Sophie and I clapped our hands in triumph. John dropped out. Birdwatching was not, he said, quite his scene. Books were his special passion, and he lacked the patience to watch birds and handle animals.

Meanwhile Sophie had been offered Mustard for the Jumping Class for Children Under Fourteen at the Frinkley Show, so she said I had better take over Caesar's training for the time being—to tell the truth she found him rather large. Chris who had now outgrown his pony and was anyway over fourteen became Sophie's coach and from mid July onwards she was more often to be found at the Langtons' farm than with me at the Hermit's place. Caesar and I grew to trust one another and, because he had no friend of his own kind, Caesar became very attached to me which was very heart warming and somehow lessened my irritation and dismay when our Mum announced that she was going to have another baby. It was a shocker and, of course, Sophie and I said stupid things like, "Why?" and "Whatever for?" which, now that I am older, I know were unkind questions to ask. It was simply

118

that we had heard so much about over-population and pollution at school, that most of us had already decided that if we married we should have only one boy and one girl each, and to see someone of our Mum's age expecting her fifth was a bit odd. Besides, it didn't seem sensible when you considered how small our house was, and secretly, I thought it would mean even less space and money for Sophie and me. But the weather was too glorious for doleful thoughts, and, after Mum had said, "I think another baby will be fun!" I jumped on my cycle and sped away down the valley to ride Caesar, deliberately pushing the thought of a new baby out of my mind, for there was nothing I could do about it, anyway.

The Hermit said Caesar wasn't arching his back enough, so we put poles on the take-off point and we made him jump several fences in a row, only nine feet apart which meant he could not put in a stride between them or flatten his back. Then I practised half-halts, leading off at a canter from a walk, and then halting and reining back in two-time, before going straight off into a canter again. These exercises were supposed to bring Caesar's hocks under him and muscle-up his hindquarters.

Out in the sun and fresh air for an hour or two every day, the Hermit's face had turned to biscuit colour; his blue eyes were steadier and would now meet mine without looking aside but not those of Marcus Davies. His hands had filled out and he had taken to wearing an old gold ring which we supposed had fallen off his fingers when they lost so much flesh and became just skin and bone. Now they were freckled and speckled with brown like a guinea fowl egg. And, although sometimes he still resembled a distraught bird, he no longer looked as though a strong wind would topple him. He was, I thought, coming out of his shell at last and, indeed, we often heard him singing to himself in his worn-out voice. Sometimes he sounded like an old 78 record being played with an over-worked steel needle on an ancient gramophone. His songs seemed to belong to the old days before hi-fi and stereo: "Keep Right On to the End of the Road," "Loch Lomond," "Down at the Old Bull and Bush", "John Peel," and then the last war songs—one about "Hanging the Washing on the Siegfried Line," the "Lambeth Walk" and those he had sung on his birthday after two glasses of champagne.

"Your Hermit is the least trendy person I have ever met," said Marcus after one of his birdwatching sessions. "He actually enjoys being thoroughly out of date and strange. I rather admire him for it."

The schedule for the Frinkley horse show came and the Hermit entered Caesar for the Novice Jumping, the very thought of which sent cold shivers of excitement down my spine. I had always avoided competing in anything, and my short sight had barred me from many activities, and now I felt as though I had jumped in the deep end before I had learned to swim. "You're mad, boy," I told myself. "Bonkers—in front of all those people . . . He'll have three refusals."

Then, just a day later, when I had put the burglary right at the back of my mind, the detective in charge of the case telephoned my father to say his men had picked up the man I saw in the café, for questioning in connection with a stolen car. Could I come to identify him? I asked Dad about an identity parade but he said I was too young to have my evidence taken very seriously. Children made poor witnesses. I said, "Excuse me, I am not a child. I am fourteen, old enough in the old days to be at sea, *and* not just a cabin boy either." Parents are odd in that way. Half the time they tell you to grow up, be your age, and so on, and half the time they refer to you as a child or, worse still, a kid, when you're actually almost a man. Dad

said the detective thought the chap with the cavalier moustache might start to talk when he saw me. He might think
the game was up *if* he were the bloke who tied me up.

It was Saturday so Dad said he would drive me over to
the station. I was glad to have him with me. He is very
big and warm, not easily rattled, and, I thought, a match
for any man.

When we reached the station we were taken into a small
bare room at the back, with just four chairs and a table,
at which the man who had been at the café sat dejectedly
tearing at his pathetic finger nails.

"That's him," I said.

"The one in the café or the one who tied you up?"
asked the detective with the bald head.

"Both."

"Never seen the boy in my life before. What game are
you playing?"

"Want us to fetch the girl behind the bar in the café.
She'll remember you. You're quite a regular, aren't you?"

"Your hands are the hands which tied me up and the
hands which lit a cigarette in the Roma, I'm sure of that,"
I said.

"I'm not the only one round here who bites his nails,
am I? It's me nerves!"

"It's not only your hands," said the detective, drawing
up his chair so that he was close to the table looking
directly across it at the young man. "He saw you in the
house when you overpowered him, when you tied him up.
He saw you then"—as he spoke the detective signalled to
me with his hand to be silent. "This boy got a good view
of you. He saw your face and all, the moustache and the
way your hair grows, your eyes, that birthmark by your
ear. He's a great boy, got his wits about him. We've got a
potential detective in this boy." The young man fell
straight into the trap.

"But he couldn't have, he . . ."

"What's that?" growled the detective, "couldn't have recognised you when you tied him up, is that what you were about to say? He says he *did* see you. He even knows how your eyebrows arch above your eyes, and he smelt your breath, too, beery it was, for you'd come straight from the Drum and Monkey just half an hour before the raid. Stoking up with Dutch courage weren't you? Before you pulled on those stocking masks."

"But if I was wearing a stocking mask how could the kid see my moustache and eyebrows, you're talking daft, aren't you. Trying to make me tell lies. Come off it!"

"So you admit you *were* in the house?"

"I haven't admitted anything, have I? You're putting words into my mouth."

"You've admitted that the boy couldn't have recognised you because when you tied him up you were wearing a stocking mask and gloves. Oh yes, gloves. Yet he saw your hands. How do you make that out?"

"Look, you're twisting my words. You're trying to make me perjure myself. I didn't say all that."

"Yes you did, innuendo."

"What's that."

"Well, by suggestion, by your reaction. You recognise the boy. You recognised him when he came into this room. I saw the light of recognition in your eye. You recognised him in the Roma Café, that's why you left before your girl had finished her meal."

"What girl?"

"The one with the hair clipped close to her head, a turned up nose," I replied, for the picture was still very clear in my mind.

"What are you talking about, that wasn't me girl friend, that was me sister."

"She wasn't a bit like you," I put in quickly.

"Well, step sister, then."

"We can soon check that. Sister in crime more likely," the detective said.

"I'm no criminal," retorted the young man nibbling at the remains of his finger nails. "You've got me all wrong. I may be out of work just now, but I'm no criminal."

"Now then," the detective began again. "You tied this boy here up in the kitchen. Tied him to a wheelback chair, that's what the boy's statement says, and the rope was stiff, right?"

"'Course it isn't right. I don't know anything about any rope. It's all double dutch to me."

"The rope was stiff and damp. It wouldn't bend, so you took off your black gloves to tie the knots and while you bent down the mask fell off."

"It nev—."

"It never," the detective finished for him triumphantly.

"I didn't say a thing. You've got nothing on me, nothing. It's all a made-up job," the young man jumped up and started to shout.

"I could see through the stocking. I could see the outline of your dark moustache," I said, really believing now that I had done so.

"That's not evidence, that's guessing. No one can see through a stocking mask, not if it's the right denier."

"Oh, so you have some experience of them, have you?" asked the detective. "You tried wearing them and you've looked at yourself in the mirror, is that it?"

"Only as a kid, all kids play cops and robbers, it's normal, isn't it?"

"But you didn't have a moustache then, so you don't really know about moustaches, do you? Please sit down again."

I felt sorry for the young man. He was trembling and

123

his eyes wore the look of a frightened animal and I saw that he was not brave at all. He sat down.

"Got a cigarette?"

The detective gave him one and lit it.

"Now, your feet are exactly the same length and width as the prints we measured in the kitchen. You may have been careful about fingerprints but you forgot about feet. And the dog, what about that poor little dog, that was a cowardly thing to do, wasn't it, beat up an old man and kick a little helpless dog's teeth in. This boy here will gladly fetch the little dog, dogs don't forget."

"I never kicked her . . . George . . ." He pulled himself up too late.

"George Blacker, yes, we know him. He's been here before. He's one of your mates, is he, the leader maybe? Gone into the picture and silver trade has he?"

"Oh give over," said the young man, taking a long pull at his cigarette.

"We'll have to charge you," said the detective, "for burglary, if not assault."

"I never hit anyone, never, not in my life."

"I'm glad of that," said the detective without conviction.

I was amazed that the man had given himself away so easily; that he appeared so frightened and inadequate, not the sort of thug I had imagined at all. I felt quite sorry for him again. He looked underfed and his eyes—I could not forget the beaten dog look in those eyes.

"Some of them are a bit thick," said the detective as we stood outside in the passage. "They see crimes on television and read about big raids on country houses and they imagine it's a piece of cake. They think so long as they wear masks and gloves, it's a cinch. They never allow for bad luck, not these young ones. They never thought you and your sister might be there. They hadn't done their homework properly, carried out a watch on the place. They just went by what they had heard, local gossip and all that. Four men against an old man with poor nerves should have been a walkover," the detective shrugged his burly shoulders. "He'll talk all right now. We've rattled him. We'll get a statement all right, and we'll pick up George Blacker, if it is *that* George and I think it is, and maybe we'll get the pictures back before long. We've got some good friends in the picture trade. This bloke and his mates are not hardened criminals yet, just small fry trying to act big. Easy to crack. They won't find it easy trying to unload a Landseer, our Art Squad is on to that."

Outside it was raining. Dad and I turned up our collars.

"Hope it won't flatten the corn," Dad said. "Quite a detective isn't he? Didn't take long to crack that young man."

I didn't say anything, for in a way I had hated it all. I don't like to see grown men cringe and I didn't want to talk about it for the time being, until I had become used to the idea.

Back at school I met Marcus, whom I called Mr. Davies except when he was at the Hermit's place, and I quickly told him what had happened.

"It was exciting but rather awful," I said.

"So the Hermit may get back his Landseer. I'm glad. I have the feeling that that picture belongs to a bit of his past which he treasures, before everything went wrong, before the war turned his world topsy turvy. I've been talking to my mother about your Hermit—you know she's a nurse, don't you? She's been interested for years in withdrawal cases. She worked in a mental hospital once, but the hours were too long, because I was just a schoolboy then and she didn't like leaving me on my own for more than an hour or so at a time."

"I don't see why people shouldn't withdraw from the

world if they want. I don't see why anyone should want to cure the Hermit," I said stoutly.

"It's not really normal for a man to isolate himself. He usually has at least a mate and the tribal instinct is still pretty strong in many of us."

"But what about the saints and the religious hermits?"

"Are you suggesting they are normal? But then it all depends on what you mean by normal," said Marcus.

We had been walking across the football pitch and the tarmac playground—or campus, if you like—and now we were at the school building itself. Marcus stopped.

"Can I come on Saturday? Do you think the old man will mind? You know there's a badger's set at the top of that copse, don't you? Right by the yew tree. I'd like to spend half the night there, and take photographs by the light of the moon. I'm sure there are some youngsters there. Maybe I'll get the pictures published."

"Yes," I said. "Do. I'm sure he won't mind. I'll ask him Saturday morning."

"I'd like to spend the whole afternoon there as well, otherwise my mother will despatch me to the launderette or something. You know how it is."

"I don't suppose the Hermit will mind," I said again, "why should he?" As I walked away up the corridor, I was aware for the first time of how we were all using the Hermit and his property for our own ends. Gradually Marcus was spending more and more time down in the field and copse, building up a photographic record of the animals and their habits; dressed in brown, his sturdy body merged with the tree trunks so that often he was hardly visible, even his beard seemed to match the rich brown of the twigs and his face, tanned by the Brazilian sun, looked as tough and golden brown as autumn cob nuts. It seemed to me now the Hermit's place had become Marcus's nature reserve, a fact he was beginning to take for granted. It was

126

his refuge from an over-loving mother and his inspiration as well as ours. Likewise, Chris and Sophie used it as a meeting place, away from their parents; it was a place for secrets and solace. It never altered, except naturally with the seasons—nature's changes in her quest to retain the biological chain about which Marcus so often lectured us.

CHAPTER NINE

SUDDENLY, too suddenly, the day of the show was upon us and all at once I was dreadfully scared. There were butterflies in my stomach and shivers down my spine and my head was spinning with thoughts of failure. Why had I ever allowed myself to be put in this position? I usually backed out of everything which might lead to a competition, let alone a public event.

Down in the dewy field the Hermit helped me groom Caesar. In the early light, straight from bed, he looked awful: hollow cheeked, yellowy-pale, his eyes mere stones thrown into dark sockets edged with purple, his teeth leaning this way and that like houses shocked by explosions waiting to be pulled down. He coughed a dozen times, a rattling old man's cough, but otherwise worked in silence with a grim determination. The pink sunrise beyond the furry line of woodland was threatened by dark clouds; the air was moist; the trees shivered in a little light-hearted breeze. The birds' dawn chorus petered out and down the valley a lone cow mooed mournfully.

I could not picture myself a horseman in a ring competing with adults. I felt about eleven. It had all been a dreadful mistake, and I wanted to back out. It isn't my scene at all, I told myself brushing a chunk of mud from Caesar's ergot. And then I wished Sophie was there, full of cheerful inconsequential chatter, which would lighten this awful seriousness which seemed to hold us in its grip. Even soldiers, I decided, do not go into battle so grim-faced; they sing or swear or make coarse jokes to lift their spirits. If I failed to complete the course it would be like a little death to the Hermit. I thought he might run back to his house and shut his door for ever and ever.

But when the sun was truly in the sky; the dark clouds falling like broken battalions away to the north, the Hermit went indoors and made a bumper breakfast of porridge, bacon and eggs, liver and sausage, toast and marmalade and a pot of strong coffee.

"We must feed the competitors," he said, handing Caesar a bucket of oats, bran, chaff and cubes. "Never enter battle on an empty stomach, rule number one."

"I think of it as a competition, a test, rather than a battle. It isn't a matter of life and death, is it?"

The Hermit went indoors without an answer.

After the meal we both felt better. There was a cheerful camaraderie between us and I stopped missing Sophie, who was down at the farm with Chris and Jane who were travelling over to the show by horse-box, an extravagance for which the Hermit refused to pay for Caesar and I.

"If a big horse like that can't jump after a ride of five or six miles, he might as well go to a knacker's yard. Besides the horse-box will remind him of the old days, when he was carted round from show to show. It might make him sour. Why," he went on, "many's the time I've ridden ten or fifteen miles to compete in a point-to-point *and* back again in the evening. But of course, that was before the war, things were different then."

After his feed Caesar was in a playful mood. He fidgeted, swished his tail, turned this way and that when we wanted him to be still, snatched his near hoof away while I was oiling it and nipped a button off my new riding coat, which was hanging on the fence. For some time the Hermit had been putting linseed oil in his feed and now his coat shone like polished mahogany and his black points like that bright coal people used to burn before the smokeless fuel came in. His eyes looked bright and healthy; his muscles rippled in the sunlight and, every so often he tossed his head in the air in a lively, defiant sort of way.

"He knows something is afoot," said the Hermit, brushing the horse's tail for the third time. "Look at him! On top of the world."

I cycled home for a wash and brush-up, the sun behind me warm on my back, the air fresh now and promising, and all around me the country wild flowers of high summer. It was lovely except for the butterflies in my stomach and the shivers in my spine.

Mum said I had been mad to take my new coat down with me and why hang it on a fence where the horse could reach it? I was fourteen now and should have more sense. Where was the button?

"Split in two. He split it with his teeth."

"So we've got to find a match. Heavens' alive and at such short notice!"

Mum fetched the botton box, in which countless spare buttons, cut off old clothes before they are put for rags, are kept.

"Mottled grey and brown," she muttered. James interrupted her; he had lost his teddy, which was once mine, and while Mum was away sorting him out, Julie tipped over the box, so that all the buttons flew this way and that. It was five minutes before I had collected them all again, but in that time I found one which almost matched those still on my coat.

E

Sophie came in with glowing cheeks. Mustard was, she said, in a wonderful mood, and his two white socks were white as untrammelled snow. His coat shone like gold and Chris had made the tack marvellously supple. She sang as she put on her white school shirt and a tie with foxes' masks on it.

"Aren't we lucky it isn't raining. Just think what it could have been like."

"Here, Matthew," Mum said. "James needs his medicine. You must finish sewing this button. Come on, don't make a face. You learned to sew at junior school, didn't you? Come on, I've made it a neck. The world's changing, the women are not going to do everything domestic any more."

"I'm afraid my rivals will all be wearing black coats and boots," I said. "Gloom all round. I shall be odd man out."

"A merry heart goes all the way", quoted our mother, firmly handing me my riding coat with the needle and thread.

Two hours later I was on the road, with Caesar's head high, his stride long and his ears hopefully pricked. He seemed in the best of moods. Little cotton wool clouds white as foam scudded across a deep blue sky, and the breeze prevented the day becoming too hot. As I came near Frinkley horse-boxes started to pass me, and then I thought about the jumps and the butterflies came back, and I thought that at fourteen I should be braver. I wasn't a junior school kid any more, even if Mum still treated me like one sometimes. In the town we met double-decker buses, huge lorries and juggernaughts, but Caesar bore himself nobly without any sign of fear. His reflection in shop windows showed a tall well-built horse, with short cannon bones and well sloping pasterns leading down to very large hoofs, a horse with a sprightly air and an endearing nose. He would, I thought, have looked well in armour, a warrior fit for Elizabethan days.

When I saw the tents and the three rings, the bunting and the long line of horse-boxes my nervousness returned ten-fold and for an awful moment I thought I might be sick. I wasn't one of those boys who are always representing their school for this or that. I was in no team, no group, no orchestra. My short-sightedness made me hopeless at games and musically my ear and voice were only rated average. My memory was unreliable, storing away information of little use to anyone but myself, and throwing out many facts and figures my teachers wished me to remember and so I was never chosen for quizzes. I had no experience of appearing before crowds of people, no practice at controlling a fluttering tummy or the shivers that ran like grated ice down my spine. And when I found my parents, Mum remarked on my paleness, "You look so tense, do relax, darling. It is supposed to be fun. Sophie is as merry as a cricket."

"I've no horse-box. Where do I tie Caesar? Has the Hermit come?"

Couldn't they see I had practical problems, that I had never been to a horse show before, not even as a spectator?

"It's an hour to go before your event, so don't worry, darling—plenty of time. Look, Sophie's over there. Do you see? Why not talk to Chris and Jane, they know the ropes."

"Chin up," said Dad.

Sophie said I could put Caesar in the horse-box while she prepared Mustard for his event. "He needs loosening up. Chris says I am to ride him quietly in large circles at the walk trot and canter. Isn't it a fabulous park?"

But Caesar wouldn't go into the horse-box. He rolled his eyes horribly, flattened his ears and swished his lovely

131

black tail. Then he reared, suddenly towering above me, a neat practised rear, as graceful as a circus horse. There was a stubborn look in his eye, which I had never seen before. This was a Caesar we did not know. It was obviously the old Caesar of his show jumping days, a Caesar I could not manage, and the very last Caesar we wanted to take in the ring at the Frinkley Show. Fearing that the horse-box would arouse all his old feelings, we gave up and tied him to a post, where he stood quite soberly swishing at flies.

Mustard looked merry and excited. He arched his neck prettily and carried his tail with a flourish, and he flexed his jaw to the bit like a dressage horse. Jane, dark haired like Chris, with an upturned nose, looked smart in a black coat. Small for her age, she had a neat compact figure with small finely cut hands. In spite of my fluttering stomach, I wondered why I had never wanted her as my girl friend, for all at once I realised that she was very pretty with a small courageous face.

Presently she was called with Sophie into the Collecting Ring, and here Mustard and Cress pranced around side by side showing off and confident because they were together. They nearly matched, both being chestnut with white stars, but Mustard had three white socks to Cress's two and his head was larger than his friend's. Both ponies were smaller than most of their rivals, which made the jumps appear rather high for them. Sophie, who had played the leading part in school plays, was used to facing the public, and looked outwardly calm, although she told me afterwards that her heart was pounding like a steam engine.

The first two ponies in her competition jumped clear rounds, which was a bit disheartening for the other competitors. Then Jane went on Cress and brought down the gate and, as they left Sophie entered the ring with Mustard letting out a long whinny to Cress. They cleared the brush fence, the gate and the wall, but took off too close to the double and brought down the second pole, so that put them level with Jane and Cress. "Horribly twinnish," said Chris, who was standing beside me.

Sophie came out smiling. It was her first show and secretly she had not expected to get round—she had seen herself falling off.

"Oh great! It was like flying, fabulous! I loved every moment. It was a lovely ride. Oh Mustard, you clever little pony! Did you see how he took the wall, wasn't he fantastic?"

"Not quite good enough to win anything, I should think, but he jumped well," said Chris soberly. "He's never jumped any better with me, anyway."

There were four clear rounds and two jump-offs, so the Langtons' ponies were right out of the running. My parents, who had also expected Sophie to fall off, beamed.

"Those fences must have been all of three feet six, quite a little horsewoman, aren't you?" said Dad. "The first time in your life, too. You were fantastic, kept a cool head on your shoulders!"

"I reckon that the Hermit must be a pretty good teacher. Am I going to meet him today, by the way?" asked Mum. "It seems unfair somehow. I've baked him pies, made him puddings, but I've never been allowed even to see him."

"Well," I began. "I don't know. I don't exactly know whether he's come, but . . ."

Then I saw him, sitting in a black car with a beaky nosed woman with rather frizzy grey hair, looking very resolute and tight-lipped, even a little mad.

"So you got here," I said going up.

"The first time out in years, yes, years," said the beaky nosed woman. "I'm his sister. You must be Matthew. This

133

is a great day for us all. I've come miles to be here, yes, miles. Dear me, I feel as though he's come back from the dead, yes, from the dead."

I was embarrassed. What could I say without speaking of the Hermit as though he were a child which he was not?

"Katie's looking well, isn't she?" I said at last as the silence was about to oppress me.

"Oh, she's found a soft pad all right, yes, she's found a nice little home and a loving master if a rather strange one," said Miss Piers in her ringing voice.

"Are you going to get out of the car?" I asked the Hermit.

"Oh, no, I should certainly fall down, palpitations, my heart."

"Nothing wrong with him, all in his imagination, yes, in his imagination, made up," retorted Miss Piers briskly, glancing at me with shrewd grey eyes. "He'll come through one day."

Come through what? I didn't like my friend being spoken of as though he was a neurotic toddler, so I asked him whether I could start loosening up Caesar, as the Novice Jumping Class was due to start in twenty minutes, and he said where was the horse? and then he said that I should not have left him tied to a post. He might break his reins. He might this very moment be trotting through Frinkley on his way home. The very suggestion filled me with horror and I ran off without another word. It was all right; Caesar was patiently standing, still tied to the post, one leg resting and a dreamy faraway look in his large eyes.

I tightened the girth before mounting. The turf was springy underfoot and Caesar calm yet lively. He walked about the showground with a confident air, his head held high. I had no doubt that he knew what it was all about.

He seemed to be living through an old, old experience all over again.

"Oh, Caesar, try, please try," I said, and I leaned down to pat his hard sleek neck.

After a time a man in a cloth cap came up to me. "Excuse me," he said, "but isn't this horse Timer, George Wheeler's horse, the one that went wrong, turned stale on him?"

"A cast-off," I replied quickly, "a throw away. Nobody wanted him."

"I swear it is or else the smitten image. Very promising he was, jumped well at Hickstead, then packed it all in, turned sour, no courage."

"Must be a different horse, Caesar has great courage."

"Never got beyond Grade C., of course," the man went on as though I had not spoken. "But George, he was hopeful, thought he had a winner. With prices what they are today he was being watched; itchy hands were reaching for their cheque books, and then suddenly . . ." he clicked his first finger and thumb together, "he packed it all in. Finished! Just like that."

"Tired of the rat race," I suggested.

"Now you're getting fanciful. Are you loosening him up for someone, you the stable boy?"

"I'm his rider," I tried to sound old and dignified. I pushed my glasses back, straightened my back.

"Bit young, aren't you? He's a big horse."

"Fourteen."

"The horse or you?"

"Me."

"I reckon old Timer must be ten or eleven now, still in his prime as a jumper."

"We have no experience. We shall have three refusals," I said. "I must go. I'm sorry. Time's getting on."

135

"Well, my mount, Sweepaway, is over there. See that dark brown with my girl on top. Great horse, but inexperienced. This is his first time."

"Good luck," I said.

"Good luck to you."

I trotted Caesar away into a quiet corner, dismounted under a chestnut tree and put my face near his.

"Please, Caesar," I said again. "Please just for today. Jump, for me and the Hermit. We're friends, aren't we? We've never let each other down, have we? And we've not overworked you, have we? We've given you an easy life with lots of affection. Please, Caesar, do you best today, just for today, I promise." Ceasar seemed to understand. He remained quite still and attentive until I had finished talking to him and then he politely nuzzled my pockets, and I found him a lump of sugar.

I remounted and rode over to speak to the Hermit.

"Dear me," said Miss Piers, "how he has filled out, not the same horse at all!"

"There's a man who says Caesar is really called Timer."

"That's right," said Miss Piers. "How strange that he should be recognised today, yes, very strange. Quite a coincidence, first time out."

"You knew?"

"Yes, didn't I write and say so?"

"Not to worry," said the Hermit. "Concentrate on the job in hand: rule number two. What was rule number one?"

"Always eat well before going into battle."

"That's right, tophole."

"Oh don't be so old-fashioned, Patrick. No one says tophole these days, nobody at all."

"I don't care; I'll say what I want. If I want to be quaint I shall be quaint."

To my surprise the Hermit now stepped out of the car, checked my girth and thoroughly inspected Caesar.

"How goes the enemy?" he asked.

"Ten minutes to three."

"Right, give him a pipe opener, a good fast canter over there, and then a couple of circles and after that just extended walking on a long loose rein. Got it?"

"Yes."

"Good. Off you go then. Don't dither. He who hesitates is lost but he who sitteth upon a pin, shall rise again." My nervousness was back, a tightness in my stomach and a faint ache in my back and the shivers, but a brisk canter raised my hopes for Caesar went well, and there was nothing rebellious or sour about him.

And then the moment had come. Our class was announced. We walked the course. My number all too soon was called. I entered the collecting ring, relieved to see that the jumps looked much lower from astride Caesar than they had when I was on foot.

A fat woman was complaining to the collecting ring steward that the show was badly run.

The man in the cloth cap was now in boots, cream breeches and a black coat. He wore a hunting tie fastened with a gold pin, and a dark blue crash cap. His brown mare wore blue bandages and a standing martingale. She seemed nervous and every so often she plunged forward swinging her head from side to side. When she was quieter the man rode up to me.

"It is Timer, I'm a dead cert. I'd know that head anywhere."

"Yes, I think you're right."

I didn't want to talk. I was looking at the ten fences and deciding how I would ride at them. They seemed high but no higher than those we had built at home. Everything depended on Caesar's mood. If he decided to opt out there was nothing I could do to make him go round. There was a simple brush fence with a guard rail, then the gate, followed by a wall, a double, a level crossing, a hog's back made with a brush and two rails, a treble, two gates placed only nine or ten feet apart and finally parallel bars. The course was built as a figure of eight with two fairly sharp turns, which is where I thought Caesar's dressage training would come in useful. The cross fat woman said it was ridiculous to end a course with parallel bars. We should have finished with a treble. The two gates she insisted were too close together. She threatened to write to the British Show Jumping Association to complain, but the collecting ring steward said he was only a steward and if she wanted to lodge a complaint she had better see the show secretary. Then the man on the brown mare was called into the ring. He cantered a circle while waiting for the whistle keeping his horse's head severely down. Then he rode her fast at the brush fence which she cleared easily; the next three jumps she took in her stride, but tossing her head from side to side she went faster and faster and when her rider turned her on the last part of the figure of eight she slipped and nearly fell. After this she lost her balance and crashed through the two gates, then refused the parallel bars. And now, even from the collecting ring, we could see that her coat was darkened with sweat and white foam lay all about her mouth. The man hit her once before putting her at the last jump again which she took at a gallop flattening her back and knocking the top rail.

When he had left the ring the cross woman on her liver chestnut went in, a picture of elegance very steady and still in the saddle. Her horse wore a jointed snaffle with a drop nose band and flexed well to the bit. She jumped a slow and careful clear round and left the ring at a balanced trot to a round of applause. She was followed by a girl on a grey in a running martingale, who jumped a fast round bringing down the front bar of the hog's back and after her, a young man with flapping arms and legs rode a flashy chestnut with four white socks, which refused three times at the treble and was disqualified, and then it was me.

I trotted in, a sea of faces and cars all around me, the shivers in my spine turning to a warm glow, the sun in my eyes and my heart thumping. I rode a circle at a canter until the whistle blew and then I put Caesar at the first fence. He sailed over, standing well back, with inches to spare, then collected himself for just a couple of strides, without being asked before going on faster again to clear both the gate and the wall. Then he came back to the bit as though he knew there would be a turn somewhere and he was waiting for the aid, and he came down the centre over the double and the level crossing. There seemed to be absolute silence as we turned again for the hog's back and then the treble where I lost a stirrup, and now there were only the two gates and the parallel bars. I tried to find my stirrup, but the next moment those two white gates loomed before me terrifyingly close to one another. I did nothing just hung on and Caesar took me over, one two— a marvellous feeling and then we galloped at the parallel bars which we cleared with a flourish, and the next minute we were leaving the ring, and people were clapping and a woman's voice cried "Well done!" Caesar took me past the collecting ring and only stopped when he reached the Hermit who had jumped out of the black car to greet us, and was clapping wildly like a small child at the circus.

"He did it all. He *took* me round. I hardly did a thing."

"A pity you weren't riding against the clock," gasped the Hermit, patting Caesar.

"Why?"

"You would be in the lead, you did a very fast round, absolutely prang-on."

"Prang on?"

"Another bit of his old war-time jargon, take no notice," advised Miss Piers.

I remembered then that she was the sister who had bossed him around in his childhood.

The man in the cloth cap came up, his smarter clothes back in the horse-box along with his horse.

"Whether he's Timer or not, I'm interested," he said.

"Interested?"

"Yeah, this isn't your father, is it? Do you ride for him? Is this Mr. Piers, the owner?" He looked the Hermit up and down with a slightly amused expression on his face. I supposed he was thinking, what a rag-bag or a proper scarecrow!

"Give you a thousand," he said. "If he passes the vet which I am sure he will do."

"Not for sale," said the Hermit. "I didn't like the way you jumped your mare, too rough."

"He's just the horse I'm looking for, with a bit of expert training, he'll make Wembley."

"No," said Miss Piers, who couldn't keep out of anything for long. "He *is* Timer and he's only jumped superbly because he likes the boy here. It's all been done by loving kindness. You would keep him at it day after day, turn him wild then strap him down with gadgets and martingales. He would spend his life on the road in a horse-box week after week. He couldn't stand it. He would turn vicious and be sold for dog meat. It's not the sort of profession he fancies for himself. He's made that clear already and he shan't be forced into it. Would you like to be a clown or a tight-rope walker or a male model?"

"The rat race," added the Hermit, feeding Caesar two

140

cubes. The man looked at the pair of them as though they were mad and indeed, they did look rather strange; the Hermit so thin and nervous; his sister birdlike, disreputable and rather fat, yet with a ringing voice which seemed to belong to a woman accustomed to having her own way.

"Two thou, if he passes the vet."

"Two thousand?" I echoed for it seemed a very large sum of money.

"Yeah, that horse has a big jump in him, the best I've seen in years. He's got quality."

"I'm told they are paying twenty thousand for jumpers on the Continent," Miss Piers replied coldly.

"Fully trained top-notchers. This one is only a novice. He's got promise, but he's not international quality yet."

"Oh, go away," cried the Hermit in a high strained voice. "Buzz off! You only see horses in terms of money; they have hearts and minds and wills of their own." He gave a gesture of extreme annoyance. "He's not for sale, I've told you, haven't I? Now quit!"

"Another clear round, a young man on a skewbald with a wall eye, aren't you watching? Don't you care?" asked Sophie, arriving on the scene. "Brother, you were fantastic, I mean it."

"Well done, son," said Dad, slapping me on the back.

"I didn't do anything. I just sat there. He simply took me round."

"You pointed him at the right jumps, you told him where to go—all those sharp turns," said Mum, struggling to keep James from patting the horses for fear that their hair or dust or something might trigger off an attack of asthma.

"This your father?" asked the man in the cloth cap, who seemed unsquashable.

"Yes, but the horse isn't his."

I couldn't bear to watch my rivals. Had I known any of them I should have been interested. As it was they were strangers who seemed to hold my fate in their hands, and the tension was too much. I buried my face in Caesar's mane and waited until my number was called.

"There's going to be a jump-off, I told you so," cried Sophie. "The liver chestnut, the skewbald and you."

The Hermit came with me to the collecting ring; he was smiling but nervous. My stomach knotted, as I saw the fences being raised. I wasn't afraid of falling off, simply that I might make a hash of things and spoil Caesar's chance's and my friend's dream.

"No," said the Hermit to the steward, "No, the horse has done his best. It's enough. We've proved our point. If we ask him to do better, he'll be ruined. Think how his mind works—the more I do, the more they ask, more and more without end, without respite. He's wise. It's his decision."

The steward looked at the Hermit as though he was mad; he looked at the old grey sweater and the out-of-date grey trousers and the old hacking jacket, with two slits at the back, which had been made for the Hermit years and years ago when he had had more flesh on his bones."

"It's *your* decision," he said. "I take it you're the owner. Let us see," he looked at a sheet of paper on his clip-board. "Mr. Patrick Piers, is that right?"

"It is."

"Is it his first show?"

"No, his last," said the Hermit looking something of a scarecrow and all at once very tired and worn.

The commentator announced that I had withdrawn and would receive the third prize and it seemed to me then that all the world was looking at me as I stood beside

Caesar by the entrance to the collecting ring. Was I sad? What did I think of it all it the eyes seemed to ask? But I didn't know the answer because I could not tell whether Caesar would have dug his toes in, reared perhaps, or taken me round a second time. I would never know and common sense told me that Miss Piers had not rescued Caesar to cast him back into the life he had grown to hate, and in my heart I thought the Hermit was right in his decision, whatever my own disappointment.

"Is he lame?" asked the woman on the liver chestnut. "He's a grand jumper. I thought you would be the winner."

"No, quite sound. He's just had enough."

"Lucky for me then," she said, agreeably. "It's an ill wind that blows nobody any good."

The skewbald knocked two fences and the liver chestnut one, and then we all went in for our rosettes and, as we cantered round, it seemed to me that I was given an extra clap; perhaps because I was younger than the other competitors or perhaps because some people in the crowd thought I was unlucky not to be allowed to jump off for first place.

When I came out the Hermit was looking rather weird; his eyes were not focussing on me and, for one terrible moment, I though he was about to suffer his long dreaded heart attack. He was flapping his arms as though they were the wings of a bird caught in a trap, and there was a hopelessness about his expression a sort of silent plea in his face which upset me. But now the photographers were around us, for we were the most local of all the competitiors in the Novice Jumping.

"The owner must hold the horse. Come on, Mr. P. Per, no, Piers, isn't it?"

The Hermit's sister pushed him forward. "Go on—your moment of glory!"

143

"Smile, Matthew, come on, *smile*," said Dad. "Cheer up!"

Caesar stood like a rock, head high but ears limp. The Hermit held one rein, squared his shoulders, and there were two red spots on his cheeks like ripe cherries, and he gave a wide smile which wasn't like any smile I had seen on any human face before. The cameras clicked. Someone muttered, "He's the recluse from down Capps Valley."

And Sophie said, "Fifty pounds; third prize fifty pounds, the exact amount we paid for Caesar. What a coincidence! It's fate, divine justice or something."

A voice behind me said: "Hi, laddie, can ye spare me a wee word?" and I turned to see a small sandy faced man looking up at me. "I need a handy lad to help me wi' the schooling. Are ye still at school or small? Are ye interested? I've two fine jumpers."

The Hermit was talking to the newspaper men, "We've achieved our goal—a clear round at the Frinkley Show, a spoiled horse reschooled. We've proved a great truth today. We've shown the world, yes the world, what patience and kindness can do," his voice was high and quavering. "He's a grand horse, one of the best, absolutely tophole."

The newspaper men were smiling as they jotted down his address in their notebooks. I imagined the headline "Recluse's horse wins at Frinkley". They were as much interested in the Hermit as Caesar.

The Scotsman was still talking, raising his voice to catch my attention.

"Ye'ld make a grand rider wi' a wee bit more practice. That your father? Yon man?"

"No, here he is."

"I'll have a wee word wi' him if ye'll not mind, no offence meant."

"Do please," I said, wonderfully self confident because I was looking down on them from Caesar's high back. The

144

newspaper men moved away. The Hermit put his arms round Caesar's neck and hugged him.

"The world's greatest horse!"

"He's started an O. Level course, rather late in the day, but you know what these boys are," Dad was saying. "I doubt that he'll have the time. He's got an awful lot of catching up to do, wants to be a naturalist. But give me your address, will you? We'll talk it over quietly at home over a cup of tea, when this little bit of excitement is over. That's right, put it on a piece of paper, that's fine. No, I won't lose it."

"Great," said the Scotsman. "Real great. I like the look of the lad, nothing bumptious about him, if ye know what I mean, a modest laddie with no airs about him, and gentle on a horse, I like that."

I won't repeat the other compliments the man paid me, they were not deserved and I was too excited to take them in at the time. Besides I was worried about the Hermit, for he seemed over-stimulated, a little wild and distraught as well as triumphant. We had worked for months for this moment and now all at once I was a little drained. I tied the yellow rosette on Caesar's brow band.

"I used to have so many of those when I was a boy," said the Hermit, "in the days before the war when everything was different. All pinned up round my bed." And then he laughed until the tears rolled down his white cheeks. And his sister said:

"Here, come on, sit in the car. Come on, I've got a nice thermos of tea in the car, yes, a nice thermos of hot tea," and she led him away by the arm.

"Always was bossy," he said, turning back to grin at me. "Always wanted to rule the roost."

But I didn't smile, suddenly I felt uncomfortable. The man was making a fool of himself, and for the first time in my life I wanted to get away from him, and it wasn't pleasant to feel like that. I watched Sophie ride in two gymkhana events—she was third in the bending—and then I set off for home, through the crowded Saturday evening streets of Frinkley, and at last I seemed to feel the extent of my triumph.

There was a warm feeling inside me, as I relived the clear round. My spirits lifted. I pushed the Hermit's wild laughing face back into the dark regions of my mind and looked to my future which seemed all at once full of hope. Marcus was going; teaching, he said, was not really his cup of tea, but he had shown me the way; for the time being he was my model. A Scotsman had offered me a job. I had jumped a clear round my first time in a show ring. My knotted stomach had untied itself in time, and I had felt no fear. I had not funked. And, best of all, perhaps I had kept my promise to Caesar: *once, only.* He was going home happy.

The sun was climbing down the horizon when we came into the valley, the birds were singing again their haunting songs of the twilight. The giant yellow threshing machines and the cutters and balers were out on the hills bringing in the golden corn, bending and packing the long stalks of straw, leaving behind great fields of creamy stubble under the red of the setting sun. And the hops? The machines for them were down the valley, too, replacing the women in headscarves and wellingtons who had come in lorries to pick this harvest by hand when I was a little child of five or six. The shadows lengthened; the little stream sparkled, caught in the last rays of the sun, and in the bright water I saw a shoal of minnows moving into the cool darkness where the boughs of an oak gave shade.

CHAPTER TEN

THE show was too much for the Hermit. Afterwards he went mad, quite mad. He ran out into the field at night in his old striped pyjamas and called on God to release him. Strange voices in his head drove him hither and thither. Demons with horned heads pursued him.

Marcus Davies found him still in his night things up a tree on the Sunday morning after the show. He took him by the arm and led him into the ivy clad house and made him tea, and put him to bed with a hot water bottle, although it was summer and a heat haze lay on the fields like the breath of a million beasts.

But the demons in the Hermit's head would not be still; they drove him out into the open again, down the stairs into the wild damp garden, and out of the rotten gate. He ran down the road, his arms flapping; his grey thatch of hair damp with sweat, his eyes wild and unseeing, and Marcus ran with him like a training coach, trying to bring him back into the real world.

We saw the pair of them, panting like lost and bewildered dogs, as they reached our house, and Dad ran out and picked up the Hermit and carried him indoors as though he were a child or an old-fashioned damsel in distress. He put him in the deep yellow armchair, and Mum made tea, while Dad rang Miss Piers, who was staying the night in a Frinkley hotel since the Hermit had refused to have her in his house. Dad caught her just before she started her journey back to her home, and, within fifteen minutes, she was on our doorstep, but when she came inside the Hermit did not recognise her, because he was in

147

his private world with the demons and for him she no longer existed. He could not be still. He ran about the room, and his struggle was terrible to see. I wanted to cry. Sophie ran upstairs and shut herself in the bathroom and Dad rang for the doctor, the fat one we didn't like very much.

"He always said it would be *too* much. Perhaps it wasn't really heart failure he feared, but madness, perhaps all the time the outside world was full of demons."

"No, he had agoraphobia and a sort of persecution mania—two things," said Miss Piers, brushing away tears. "He was a prisoner in Singapore, with the Japs. He suffered. He worked on that terrible railway. I forget its name. You know the prisoners had to build it, to work like navvies in the hot sun with hardly any food; when they collapsed they were left to die like flies, and they were hit if they did not work hard enough. It was all terrible and brutal, yes, brutal. The Japs beat them, yes, the Japs beat them. Some went blind later from the blows, their eyes unjelled. Do you know what I mean? Do you understand? Many of those who survived had nervous breakdowns later, some twenty years later. Some are still in hospital. Man's brutality to man is worse than anything the animals do to each other, yes, much worse. This is *his* breakdown. It's been like a boil swelling and festering for nearly twenty years and now it's burst, yes, now it's burst."

"His wife, son—Nigel?" I asked.

"That was the awful thing, through all his suffering he kept a picture of them in his mind. If only he could survive eventually Britain would win and he would be home, but then . . ." she cried a little, mopped her eyes, "he came back to find them dead, his home gone, destroyed by bombs. He came back to nothing but a tired country and his sister who always had irritated him; yes, his sister, with whom he shared nothing but a love of animals. It was too much. Can you see? It was too much. He wanted to creep away to die. He had seen and felt too much. He wanted to hide his face from man's cruelty to man. He didn't want to be hurt any more. He was a war hero, yes, a war hero, a casualty of war. He should have been given a medal, but no one took much notice of him. They were too busy rebuilding the country, getting rich again, yes, too busy."

Marcus Davies came in then. "Can anyone sit with him? I want to phone my mother. She's a nurse. She has a way with invalids. Be kind to him. He's in deep fear. I think he believes he is with the devil. Someone must hold his hand." Dad went. The Hermit was in the kitchen crouched in the corner like a trapped animal; he was shaking all over and beads of sweat stood out on his forehead, yet his skin was deathly white and his eyes stared in terror from their purple sockets. I didn't want to see him like this. It was too private and terrible. I didn't want him to know that I had witnessed such humiliation.

Miss Piers was behind me, sniffing into her handkerchief.

"I thought the horse would help," she said. "I thought you children had done him so much good. You seemed to give him a purpose for living. He was so alive yesterday, yes, *alive*. He cared about something again. When I fetched him from his house he was smiling—my heart nearly burst with happiness—and everything went so well just how he wanted it, yes, just how he wanted it. Of, dear, life is a very strange thing."

Mrs. Davies came before the doctor. Plump and kindly and surprisingly young, considering Marcus was in his twenties, she spoke with a slight Irish brogue in a voice soft as a gently flowing river, and she radiated calm. When she entered the kitchen we all stood back, sensing the arrival of an expert. She went straight to the Hermit and held his hand.

"All right, my love," she said, looking into his face with the kindest pair of eyes imaginable. "Steady now. It's all going to be all right. You're coming back into the light of day, sure, you're coming through. The devil's with you and no mistake, but he's going away like a leaf on the wind. He'll not be staying. Calm now, you're strong; you're a fighter, Patrick Piers, a great fighter. No devil is going to beat a man like you. But it may be a struggle, a long, long struggle, but you've got to go through with it, that's your fate just now, but you shall not be deserted. Come now sit on this chair. There now, we'll make you comfortable and those demons will lose heart. Come now, a good cup of strong, sweet tea."

The Hermit stared at her, and his eyes softened; he lost the wild fear in them, which had been so terrible to see.

"Have you come, have you come, my saviour?" his voice was hardly above a whisper.

"I'm just helping you through this rough old time," said Mrs. Davies.

He obeyed her absolutely. His trust in her was uncanny.

He was obediently drinking tea when Dr. Sanders came, fat-faced and complacent as ever, a black case in his hand.

"They always choose a Sunday for this kind of caper," he said.

And then Sophie and I were told to go outside to "play" in the garden, as though we were six years old.

"He will recover," I said desperately. "Of course he'll recover. Wasn't Marcus's mother fantastic?"

"I didn't see," said Sophie. "I couldn't bear to watch."

*   *   *   *   *

Dr. Saunders quietened the Hermit with an injection and then Dad drove him to Frinkley Hospital, while Mrs. Davies stayed holding his hand.

Dad said afterwards that the Hermit had not wanted to leave Mrs. Davies, that he hung on to her as though she was all he held dear in the world, as though he would die without her. But once he was in hospital the injection had come into full effect and he had drifted away into sleep.

"They will take care of him. He's in the best place," Dad assured us. "Now we must look after the animals."

"Terrible what war does," Mum said. "The after-effects go on for so long. They say the children who were evacuated from London have problems now, which no one ever dreamt of at the time."

But Sophie and I were tired of tragedy and talk of war; we made our own sandwiches and went out on our cycles for the day. We wanted to get away from it all, to breathe fresh air in the hills and search the new stubble for voles and dormice. We needed to forget at least for a time.

We were not allowed to visit the Hermit, for which secretly we were glad. For a month only Mrs. Davies visited him. Marcus told us that the Hermit was going through a kind of hell in hospital, but that there was a marvellous young psychiatrist there, who believed that the Hermit must pass through fire to become whole again.

The Hermit was to receive no electric shock treatment, no deep-sleep drugs. He had to experience his madness to the full. The hell was necessary if the Hermit were to recover; it was nature's cure for all the suffering he had endured while building that infamous railway in the hot sun of the Far East. It was essential, Marcus said, that the Hermit should face the demons. Just as dreams were necessary so that at night we could experience the problems we feared through the sub-conscious, so now the Her-

151

mit must go through this dream world if he were to regain his sanity.

"It's all a new theory," Marcus said. "But it sounds logical, doesn't it? Well, feasible, anyway!"

The treatment was experimental and Mrs. Davies, lonely since her husband's death three years earlier, had longed for a challenge. She was a woman, Marcus explained, who needed to be needed. So she struggled with the psychiatrist to bring the Hermit through his ordeal back into the real world. She worked in the mornings regularly at a clinic, but she spent much of every afternoon and evening with the Hermit, even visiting him when he spent a few hours in a padded cell.

"I will save that man if it kills me," she announced. "He's done no one any harm, only served his country and suffered for it, and received scant gratitude."

We rode Caesar now and then, but somehow, the pleasure of these rides were tainted with the Hermit's madness and for me the goal had gone.

A month later the Hermit was allowed home on the condition that Mrs. Davies stayed with him, and so she moved into the big front bedroom and Marcus moved into a small back bedroom, saying his presence was needed to prevent unseemly gossip about a widower and widow setting up a home together without being married. The Hermit was put in his own bedroom, with a view of the field and, as the days shortened and the autumn mists lay on the crisp October leaves, Marcus started to feed Caesar for Sophie and me.

It seemed to us to be the end of an era. The Hermit and the house were no longer ours as we had once felt them to be. Sadly, while we continued to ride Caesar at week-ends, we saw the ivy clad house change its character and lose its mystery as Mrs. Davies scrubbed and cleaned and Marcus cut back the rampant climbers and mended the rotten doors and windows. It began to look tidy, occupied and tended. And a lawn began to take shape in the garden and an arch was built for the rambling roses which had sprawled through the grass, a tangled mass of flowers, a sweet scented carpet, the like of which we had seen nowhere else. The gates were repaired, creosoted or painted; the barn's missing tiles were replaced, creating a patchwork roof, for the old ones could not be matched.

Marcus continued to teach at our school four afternoons a week until a permanent teacher could be found.

"I'm not really a teacher," he said. "I do all the wrong things like letting you call me Marcus instead of 'Sir,' or 'Mr. Davies.' I can't be bothered with the little tyrannies and all the rules and sticking to a time-table. If I take a class on a project I need at least two hours, not a mere forty minutes."

He told us mothering was his mother's *career*. She was like the sort of hen who takes every lost chick under its wing! "She spoiled me terribly when I was a small boy. I wonder that I ever broke away," he said. Nursing was for her a vocation, a part of life she would not be without; she needed to tend the sick and rescue the lonely or she felt only half alive. Miss Piers had begged her to become resident nurse to the Hermit, whom she wanted out of hospital. "And I'm the chaperone," he added, laughing, but he was really glad to be away from the modern house on the new estate, to be, as he said, in the heart of a miniature nature reserve. His photographs of the nesting woodpeckers had already been published in a nature magazine and now he was researching into the living and mating habits of the moles which tunnelled so industriously in the Hermit's field.

Just before Christmas the Landseer came back, for the thieves had been unable to unload it on anyone and had eventually left it in a telephone kiosk. The Georgian teapot, jug and sugar bowl were found for sale in Portobello Market, London, but the rest of the silver had either been melted down or shipped to the continent. The four burglars, all now caught, were each sentenced to two years' imprisonment.

As the holly shone bright with scarlet berries and the hedges with hips and haws, the Hermit was to be seen on fine days taking a little walk down the lane on the arm of his faithful nurse. And, all at once, the name Hermit seemed no longer to fit that sturdier body and well fed face. We began to think of him as Mr. Piers, a rather forbidding gentleman with a nose like a general's. In reality, he looked very like a stray animal which has found a good home; fatter, sleeker and contented. The devils had gone, the demon voices faded into thin air as the early mists go with the sunrise. When we spoke to him he seemed an ordinary person, who occasionally used uncommon words and jargon from the nineteen thirties. Sometimes his attention would stray from our anecdotes and stories to Mrs. Davies; the two of them would exchange glances as though they had a special language of their own or a secret understanding. Gone were the days of hot Bovril, lemonade and all those biscuits. Gone the strangeness of the house; the excitement of not knowing how the Hermit would be from day to day.

Then, just before Christmas, on a day of swirling mists and wild, blinding rain, Dad dropped his bombshell. We were, he said, about to move to the other side of Frinkley. With a new baby soon to arrive we needed a larger house and this had been found.

"What's it like?"

"Where? Is it old?"

"Or new?"

We were full of questions.

154

"Hop in the car, we'll go and see it right now," he said.

It was Victorian, one of a pair, with gables and frowning windows, and inside three arches, panelled door and moulded ceilings. It was shabby and yet there was something rather grand about it, the atmosphere perhaps, for we knew at once that this house had a past. It was quite different from a new place. There was a cellar and there were attics looking across fields.

"Please note there's a riding school next door. It's one of the reasons why we decided to buy," Dad said. "The mortgage will be rather large, but I'm much nearer the Mill, that will save petrol."

"If you want to take up that Scotsman's offer in the spring you will be just six miles nearer to his stables," added Mum, but I knew I wouldn't because he had wanted me every day for at least two hours and I had at last set my heart on going to university to read botany and zoology. Marcus had been replaced by a quiet pipe-smoking biologist who liked project work and gave us all great scope for using our initiative. His arrival and his teaching strengthened my resolve, although he could never quite fill the gap Marcus had left. I knew now that I could not spare two or three hours every day if I were to gain good O. Level results.

"Perhaps I can help at the riding school," I suggested. "We're going to miss Caesar."

"You can do your woodwork in the cellar and your homework in the attic. We thought you might like a bed sitting room at the top of the house, Matthew. There will be loads of room for the new baby, and look at the garden, walled—isn't it great? Do you see the fruit trees and the green house?"

"Will we have to change schools?" asked Sophie.

"Not at all, not at all," said Mum brightly. "I've been

155

in touch with the Education Department about that. You can both stay where you are. It's better for you, Sophie, isn't it—only a little bus ride. Matthew will have fifteen minutes to go on his bike."

Our parents were trying to sell the place to us; they were closely watching our expressions, hoping to placate us if we suddenly started to wail, but, all at once, we saw that a move was the best way out. We all needed a change before the new baby came. Our life at the Hermit's place had become tepid and unsatisfactory, no more than a pale imitation of the days we had spent there before the Frinkley Show. We saw that we needed to get away from the Hermit before we could see his new point of view and grow to like Mrs. Davies.

So we moved in in the New Year, just after the Hermit married Mrs. Davies very quietly in a Roman Catholic church, and Marcus left to work on a nature reserve on a North Sea island, and Miss Piers sent Caesar a donkey to keep him company so that he would not miss us very much. We shed a few tears, for it is sad to leave the house in which you have been born, and we loved that valley which, sometimes, because of its isolation, seemed almost to be our own. Its secrets were our secrets and each year we had made new discoveries about the birds and the flowers, the trees, the insects, the reptiles and the fish that lived on its riches and in its shade. As Dad drove us away following the huge removal van which was bearing our belongings to our new home, we dared not look back for fear that we would let out great sobs of sorrow, for we thought ourselves too old to cry.

But our Mum wept and she did not care who saw her tears tumbling down her cheeks like rain from leaky gutters.

"We came here after our honeymoon. It was my dream

house, those little dormer windows . . . I've been so happy there."

"We were in a rut," Dad said. "It's good to make a change. We must move on. Time doesn't stand still. Cheer up, my love."

The riding school was run by two sisters, tall, slim girls with thick, fair hair and limpid blue eyes which disguised strong wills and obstinate natures. They were twins, horse mad, merry and very good instructresses. They allowed me to help whenever I liked and, after a bit, they paid me for my work by letting me ride for nothing when anyone cancelled a lesson and there was a pony or horse free. They took part in all the local shows and indeed had seen me jump at Frinkley and amongst their other helpers was a boy around my own age, who hoped to join the army. Before long he and I were fast friends.

Farther up the road, a tile-hung house looked through apple orchards into wooded slopes of oak and hazel, walnut and yew, and here Sophie found a new friend in a girl called Amanda, who rode a grey called Mermaid and owned two cavalier spaniels named Donald and Flora. So, while I was at the riding school, Sophie was usually with Amanda, and in this way we started new lives for ourselves.

*　　*　　*　　*　　*

One cold day in the dentist's waiting room, idly turning the leaves of a magazine, while imagining the ordeal to come, I saw a photograph of the Hermit's Landseer illustrating a learned article on that artist's work. And all at once I was filled with nostalgia for the days which were past. I longed to see the Hermit and his horse and our dear friend, Kate, again, to go down that enchanted valley, over the hump-backed bridge with the mist moist on my face and the early sun lighting the pearly sky with

157

gold. I wanted to feel the air of the place, to smell those
country scents and, now that I had become a poetry lover,
Meredith's lines ran through my head, haunting me.

"Lovely are the curves of the white owl sweeping
    Wavy in the dusk lit by one large star.
Lone on the fir-branch, his rattle note unvaried,
    Brooding o'er the gloom, spins the brown evejar.
Darker grows the valley, more and more forgetting:
    So were it with me if forgetting could be willed.
Tell the grassy hollow that holds the bubbly well-spring,
    Tell it to forget the source that keeps it filled."

I told Sophie.

"I feel exactly the same, how funny. Let's go. Why
not?" she asked. "They probably wonder why we never
go. Caesar must wonder."

"I'm not sure that horses *do* wonder," I said.

So the very next Sunday Sophie and I made ourselves
sandwiches and, after helping Dad with the washing up,
and the potato peeling for the others' lunch, we mounted
our cycles and rode the eight miles through Frinkley, past
our old house which looked strangely small compared
with our Victorian place, and down into that beloved valley, where a sharp wind from the hills blew our hair hither
and thither, and brought the first scents of spring from
the woods we knew so well. There had been changes; a
bungalow was raising its red bricks by the hump-backed
bridge to stare across the stream with steel framed windows; an oak lay sadly on the verge, its sapless branches
splayed out on hoary grass; and, farther on, a thorn hedge
once the home of many a sparrow and proud speckled
thrushes, had been mown down and replaced with wire,
which made us seethe with rage.

But the largest change of all lay in the refurbishing of

the Hermit's place. A gravel drive led now to a white-painted front door flanked by two elegant bay trees in teak tubs. Winter jasmine freed from countless weeds lay green against the walls, and yellow forsythia bloomed, dripping beads of bright amber down creosoted trelliswork. Re-painted, repointed, half stripped of the ivy's stranglehold, the house seemed to smile with a new face across the lane over the patchwork of fields up towards the woods which ran along the ridge of hill against the grey blueness of the horizon. The birds still sang almost without pause, and the honeysuckle rambled in the high thorn hedges as before, and everywhere there was that air of peace which had so captivated us a year ago.

The Hermit came to the door to greet us, standing be-side his wife, shy, but smiling, tanned from a holiday in the Canary Islands. He looked younger, years younger, and his eyes, like the place, looked at peace. Caesar whin-nied when he saw us and came with long strides to the gate. He nuzzled our pockets with his long mobile upper lip, then nibbled our cheeks breathing warm air into our faces. We gave him lumps of sugar, and then, as though suddenly remembering his manners, he turned to nuzzle Rebecca, the little grey donkey, who had joined him at the gate. Perhaps he was trying to say to us, "See, I have a friend. I'm not lonely." Or is that too fanciful an explana-tion?

Katie, plumper, feathery tail wagging gently, her tortoise-shell face smooth as velvet, licked our faces then offered us her paws.

"You see, you are not forgotten," the Hermit said.

"You will stay for lunch, won't you?" suggested his wife, touching Sophie's hair with her ministering, nurse's hands.

All at once we were sure that everything had turned out for the best, that our friendship for the Hermit could not have continued as it was, that nothing in life remains the same, that perhaps most people are meant to live in couples, not alone.

We went home much later surprisingly happy, the March air sharp in our faces; the sky pale as opals, to find an empty house, the door locked, the key under the mat. Our Mum had gone. James and Julie had been dumped with the neighbour—a woman, with four children, whose husband worked for the railways.

"Her time has come. She's early. The pains started soon after you left. Your Dad's at the hospital," the woman said. "Better take the little ones back now, give them their tea. The boy's a bit weepy-like."

The house seemed very empty without our parents, almost like a place stripped of pictures and furniture. Silently imagining the pangs of childbirth, wondering exactly how the baby would come, we gave James and Julie milk, bread, butter, honey and cake. We could not eat ourselves. We looked at one another and fidgeted and made disjointed conversation.

An hour later Dad telephoned from the hospital to say that our Mum had been delivered of a seven pound baby girl, Melanie Jane, and that both were doing well.

"I shall have to go straight to the Mill now. I'm on tonight. Can you put the little ones to bed? I'll slip back half way through the shift to see how you are. All right?"

"Right," we said, and, "Give our love to Mum."

And so for us a new life and a new era began.